North of Juárez, Far from Saigon

Connie Beckett

Flint Hills Publishing

Cover Design by Amy Albright

Flint Hills Publishing
Topeka, Kansas
Tucson, Arizona
www.flinthillspublishing.com

Printed in the U.S.A.

Paperback Book: 978-1-966323-34-1
Electronic Book: 978-1-966323-35-8

Introduction

This story, and the town of Kingston, is fictional but it is based on a real situation. In the 1980s, meat packing plants were built in the middle of the United States, including the Kansas towns of Garden City, Dodge City, and Emporia. Meatpacking work was hard and gruesome but paid above minimum wage. The processing plants hired Mexican and Central American immigrants as well as refugees from Vietnam after the end of the Vietnam Conflict.

The population of the rural and largely white communities boomed with people from different countries and cultures. The result was high housing costs, poverty, displacement, crime, and often hostility from long-time residents. Schools had to quickly adapt for students who spoke a foreign language and had social needs. Many of the Hispanic workers were illegal and the Immigration and Nationalization Service (INS) periodically conducted raids.

In the 1980s my hometown of Garden City experienced many of these changes. I'm proud of the way the city worked to assimilate its new citizens. Decades later I can still hear multiple languages spoken, see signs written in three languages, visit the expanding Asian exhibit at Lee Richardson Zoo, and sample the great variety of Hispanic and Asian foods in restaurants and supermarkets. When I visit the cemetery to lay flowers on Memorial Day, I can trace the history of the town from the older sections with their European surnames to the more recent sections interspersed with the gravestones exhibiting Asian and Hispanic surnames.

Of course, this change did not occur without problems. Many long-time residents were not supportive of its new residents believing that the benefits of community growth did not outweigh the social problems the workers brought with them. What I seek to do in this novel is to demonstrate that humans all have the same need to belong and be respected. Despite our differences, we must continue to work together to make our communities strong.

Curtis

—◇—

Kingston, Kansas, Summer, 1984

It was the end of July, and the tiny, windowless office was a sauna. Curtis pulled a tissue from the box on his desk and wiped his brow. There was barely enough room for his desk, never mind the wobbly metal table where Alicia worked. The copy machine and filing cabinets sat outside the office, and he knew Alicia took every opportunity to escape and file or cover for the receptionist.

This left Curtis wedged in a corner—his desk, and the bulky computer terminal sitting on top, a barrier between him and the door. He looked at the wall clock. It showed 4:10. A click sounded with every jerk of the second hand, a nagging reminder that the grant application he was reviewing had to be completed and in the mail before the post office's last 5:45 pick up time.

His stomach burned. Curtis opened the desk drawer for the bottle of antacids. Before he could pop one in his mouth, he heard the soft clicks of beads on beads. A young Latina girl, six or seven-years-old he guessed, entered the office. Her sleeveless white blouse made her brown skin appear even darker. Today, the dark hair had been twisted into thin long braids that ended with beaded rubber bands. Head down, she glanced at Curtis out of the corner of one eye. Then she turned, her head lifted, and she beamed a white-toothed smile at Alicia.

"Hello, Mrs. Rodriquez," the girl said.

"Well, hello to you too," Alicia said.

Curtis ignored the girl. He focused on the papers in front of him and tried to appear too busy to acknowledge her. Every day, this girl came and bothered them. Didn't she understand the time and work involved in running a community youth center like this? He and Alicia had work to do, especially today. It was hard enough scheduling staff and volunteers, and making sure expenses were justified for the approval of their board of directors. Was it also required of him to suffer this daily interruption?

"We're really busy now," he said, hoping to dissuade the girl. He saw a flicker of uncertainty before the girl turned from him and shot another smile at Alicia. Curtis realized he had lost this first skirmish in the battle for Alicia's time.

"How was your day?" asked Alicia.

"It was excellent," the girl said.

"This is movie day, isn't it? Did you and the other kids go to see a movie?"

"Yes, we saw the new movie about a space alien. E.T. call home," she said in a deep growl. "Elliott was sad when their friend left in the spaceship, but E.T. was sick and he had to go home."

Occasionally, the girl would flit her eyes toward Curtis. He knew she did because he could hear the clack of the beads that hung off the braids when her head turned. Curtis cleared his throat, the sound in the close room making both Alicia and the girl jump. He couldn't recall the girl's name. Shantella or Marceluna or something like that. He turned over a page of the still incomplete grant application to proofread the next page.

"I got a hundred percent on my spelling words today," the girl, whatever her name, said.

"My teacher, Mrs. Nguyen, she said I had the best score in class. She gave me a star. Look."

Curtis glanced at the paper the girl held out to Alicia. The childcare department ran a summer learning program, and the page she held was lined, just like the tablets he had used in elementary school. Wide-spaced lines on the paper were separated by dotted lines signifying how tall the small letters should be. Sure enough, there was a big, shiny gold star in the upper right-hand corner. He leaned over his desk and tried to read the name under the star. His chair squeaked, and the girl quickly brought the paper down and turned her back to him. Alicia glared at Curtis. He pointed to the application.

Alicia ignored him and turned back to the girl. "Congratulations," she said. "Those look like big words."

The girl responded with an even broader smile.

"They are. I had to study hard. I'm reading a hard book too. It's about this beautiful, brave horse named Black Beauty. He grows up in the country with his family, and then has to leave his family and go to work. I know how to spell carriage. C-A-R-R-I-A-G-E. It's sad sometimes."

Curtis recalled his daughter reading the book. How old was Melody when she read it? He couldn't remember. Last year in fourth grade, perhaps. And the girl, how old was she? Six or seven? Eight? He still couldn't recall her name. It was something musical ending with a soft vowel sound. Sophianna? No, that wasn't right. It was a name that sounded made up. Didn't anyone anymore name their children ordinary names like Janet or Sheryl? No, they had to create some misspelled and unpronounceable name out of thin air that would forever follow their child like a heavy stone on a chain.

His own daughter's name was Melody. It was a nice name that people could pronounce, a name that wouldn't cause her to be teased by the other kids. His daughter Melody with the heavy feet and her mother's flat voice. Well, as least Melody was a name that could shape her as she grew. Now what was this little girl's name? Was it Sharony or Marquisa? He couldn't recall.

"That sounds very interesting," Alicia said.

Curtis tapped a pen against the desktop and concentrated on sending a silent message to Alicia to rush their conversation toward its end. He knew from similar encounters with this persistent child that if a word or phrase about their lives outside the club slipped out, it would invite endless questions. Then, this daily exchange would go on even longer and he would be even further delayed. He glanced at the clock. It now showed 4:28. He glared at Alicia, but she ignored him. They huddled together, as if trying to carve out a refuge in the airless space.

"Well, guess we'd better get back to work. Gotta get this done," Curtis waved the pages of the application in the air between them, "or you won't have a place to come to after school."

The girl's smile faltered. Alicia glared. Curtis felt a tingle of happiness.

"No club?" the girl asked.

The tingle of happiness faded as Curtis realized this had only opened the door to more useless talking. He looked at the clock. It read 4:29.

"Go on, go on." He waved his hand in a shooing motion toward the open door. "Leave now so we can finish this."

Curtis picked up the pen and started reading the narrative. He rested a hand against his brow to block further conversation. For a wondrous moment there was silence. He listened for the patter of feet making toward the door but heard only the soft sound of the rotating fan as it moved the hot air. He crossed out "there" on the page and replaced it with "their." Couldn't these people grasp the basics of English?

"I don't think the center will close, honey," Alice said, patting the girl's bare, brown shoulder. She faced Curtis, her eyes sharp. "Isn't that right?"

Both were looking at him now. Two sets of brown eyes, one set hard and the other uncertain.

Hrump. Curtis' left eyelid started twitching. He pressed two fingers against a disobedient eyelid, hoping pressure would stop the twitch, and tried to read. He still didn't hear movement toward the door. The fan swiveled, moving time closer to the deadline.

"Come on, honey," Alicia said to the girl. "Let's go get us a Coke, find some better company."

"Yeah, good idea," Curtis said, his voice louder than he intended.

"Mr. Myerson?" said a quavering voice.

Curtis pretended he couldn't hear. Damn, she was persistent. If he ignored the girl, maybe Alicia would just take her and leave. He read a sentence and read it again, not making sense of it. He knew they were still in the room, he could hear them breathe and the periodic click of the girl's beads.

He looked up. The girl stood trembling, Alicia had her hands on her hips.

"What is it?" Curtis asked.

"Where do I go if you close the club?" the girl asked.

"You go home like everyone else."

"But...."

"But what?" He was losing the last bit of his patience.

"No one's home. My mom works late. Antonio is...." She stopped talking, lips in a thin narrow line. She looked up at Alicia. Alicia put a hand on her back trying to turn her toward the door, but the girl stood firm.

Curtis said, "Antonio's your older brother, right? I know he doesn't work. Why can't he watch you?"

"I don't like Antonio's friends. They're mean. They...." She stopped.

Curtis had heard rumors about Antonio—the street level drug dealers he ruled, the unsolved shootings he was rumored to have engineered. There was also the sporty Pontiac Trans Am that Antonio drove with flashy chrome wheels, a stereo system with bass speakers that rattled the center's windows, and a blue pearl, custom paint that refracted light into hard shards.

"Listen, maybe the club won't actually close," he said. "But if we don't get this done, it might. We'll be out of money, and I'll be out of a job."

"But, Antonio," the girl said.

Curtis shooed them toward the door. "If you don't go, Mrs. Rodriquez and I can't get the application done. And, if we don't get the application done, we'll lose our funding. If we lose funding, the club closes. And why? Because you're talking so I can't get it done."

"Come on, honey," Alicia said. She placed a hand on the girl's head pushing her toward the door. As she left, Alicia glared at Curtis.

Curtis looked at the clock once again—4:39. He groaned and turned back to his work. One page left to proof, and then he'd call for Alicia. She'd correct the errors, make copies and then, finally, he would be able to rush the envelope to the post office in time for the last mail pick up. He was glad Alicia was making the changes and not the work-study intern. The intern would have laboriously moved her fingers across the keyboard, now and then looking up a word in the Spanish-English dictionary she kept beside the outdated, donated, word processor.

At last, he reached the end. The clock showed 5:03.

"Alicia," he called loudly. There was no answer. Was she still with that girl? "Alicia," he tried again. Still no answer.

Curtis walked around the corner to the receptionist desk. There he found Alicia, sitting very still and staring out the glass door at the street.

"Didn't you hear me call you?" The reception area was quiet, so he knew she had once again ignored him.

"Here's the app narrative," Curtis said. "I marked the corrections."

"You upset Marcela," she said. She remained still, gazing out the center's door.

"Who?"

"Marcela."

"Oh, the girl. You knew we didn't have time for her today."

Alicia finally faced Curtis. For a long minute, she just stared at him.

"That's all?" she asked.

"Every day that kid pesters us. I can't get anything done."

Alicia glared, not saying a word.

"I just need this done so I can get it in the mail." Curtis held out the file with the application tucked inside. Alicia didn't take it.

She said, "That kid, as you call her, was almost in tears when she left your office."

"All I told her was the center might close if I don't get this mailed and...."

Alicia's eyes narrowed.

"This place is more than a daycare to her. It's Marcela's home. Director Kline always made time for her. She comes to see us every day because she wants us to like her, give her a little attention. Can't you see that?" She searched Curtis' face. "Oh lordy, you can't. Marcela's mom works two jobs so she can pay for her Catholic school tuition. She does that because she wants to keep her daughter safe, give her a chance. She already lost a baby daughter to SIDS and a son to a drunk driver."

"Well, if Antonio would get a job."

"Well, the streets got to Antonio. He's no saint. Maybe his momma lost him too. I know what people say, but that boy loves his little sister. That's why he's here every day to pick her up. Every day."

An easy obligation for Antonio since he doesn't work a real job, Curtis wanted to say, but he knew it would further alienate Alicia, and he couldn't afford more delays. Instead, he once again held out the file. This time, Alicia grabbed it.

Curtis sat at his desk and waited for Alicia to finish. The clock read 5:20. Finally, he heard the printer outside the office begin to whirr. Twenty minutes. He could still make it. Then he could go home to his apartment and forget about this place for a while. First thing he'd do is fix a sandwich. Today, it's sliced, smoked ham with Provolone cheese and mayonnaise, the real kind of mayonnaise that his ex-wife didn't like and had never bought. Then, he'd add some potato chips, no, make it carrot sticks. He'd sit on the folding chair in the tiny apartment, eat his supper, and watch the local news. Then, and this was the best part of his day, he would make the one drink a day he allowed himself.

He'd gone to the AA meetings he was required to attend. Men and women, some old and some young, would each take a turn saying how booze or pills, or whatever, had ruined their life. How one drink was too many and a thousand weren't enough. He had even stood once and told the group, yes, he had gotten drunk and picked a fight. Okay, more than once, and now he realized he was just a drunk, had no control over alcohol. He said it, but he didn't believe it. He had lost his job and his marriage in two short months. Who wouldn't drink in those circumstances? Before his life hit the crapper, he'd have a couple of beers or cocktails at home, or when he and his ex-wife, Amy, went out. He'd had no problem with it. No, he wasn't an alcoholic. Alcoholics had no control. His little incident at the bar was the result of circumstances.

After he finished supper, he'd take out his favorite tumbler, squat and wide with a thick glass bottom and faceted sides. First, he would hold the glass up to the light and watch as the prisms distorted his view of the flimsy kitchen cabinets. Next, he'd take out the bottle of Glenlivet single malt scotch he kept in the cabinet next to the kitchen sink. He'd pour two shots over ice, no more and no less, carefully measuring each shot. He'd swirl it, ice cubes clinking, vapors from the scotch already soothing him.

The printer stopped whirring, and he heard Alicia's footsteps, the rustle of papers and footsteps again as she walked back to the reception desk. Curtis turned off his computer and rose, patting his front pocket to make sure he had his car keys. He turned off the office light and was closing the door when he heard muffled voices and then loud pops.

"What the hell?" he said.

Alicia screamed.

2

Rochelle

A cross the street from the Kingston Community Center, Rochelle Castro Sanchez sat at the front of her store, between the plate-glass windows and the counter where the register stood. From there, she was able to watch both the street and any customers browsing in the store. She turned a page of *Vogue* magazine. Rochelle alternated between looking at *Vogue's* leggy blondes as they leaned against a white adobe wall in their short dresses and red heels, and the sidewalk outside her store.

One of her storefront's tall windows had a crack in the upper corner where a pellet round, energy spent by distance or velocity, had hit it. The pellet pecked a chip out of the glass and sent a single ray of break toward the corner. The heavy glass windows were expensive, and Rochelle hoped the seasonal change from hot, dry heat to shuttering cold wouldn't make the crack worse. Sometimes, when the sun hit the glass just right and she wasn't busy, Rochelle watched the crack gather the light. First, the sun illuminated the line, making it glow with a life of its own. When the sun moved, the light winked out, the line becoming nearly invisible again. She had read somewhere that glass was neither a solid nor a liquid but something in between. How did that work? When her bones eventually turned to dust, would the glass pane on its slow slide to the floor finally pull the crack apart?

She sighed and turned back to the magazine. Damn, it was hot today. Heat waves shimmied off the tops of cars in the lot across the street at the community youth center. Black asphalt in the street had softened in the sun, and it sucked at shoes and tires. Rochelle lifted a sheet of long black hair, letting the soft breeze of the ceiling fan cool the back of her neck. She pulled a tissue out of the box and dabbed it across her chest and between her breasts, where a bead of perspiration tickled. She was proud of the high roundness of those breasts. It had taken her three long years of swallowing hormone pills and saving money before she could afford the implants.

There was still the final surgery, necessary to complete the change from the boy she had been born to the woman she always knew lived inside. She had the money tucked away, but time seemed to click from one day into the next without action. She breathed deep and stretched, feeling the muscles in her back tense and relax. Maybe, it was just her fear of how the dynamics of pleasure would change that held her back. She pulled the cotton skirt high on her thighs and let the breeze from the ceiling fan drift across her bare legs.

She could smell the dried herbs and roots tucked into their tidy bins on the wall behind her. She had found the bank of old apothecary drawers in a classified ad when she first opened the shop. The ambiance of a wall of six-inch square oak drawers, each with an oxidized brass pull, gave value to the substances inside: herbs, leaves, roots, and dried mushrooms nestled in cotton drawstring bags. Rochelle mixed and sold potions to immigrants living in the city from the old countries—Vietnam, Cambodia, Mexico, Colombia, and El Salvador. They knew the power of the natural blends that soothed sore skin, calmed internal organs, and repaired broken hearts long before white Europeans traveled to America from across the sea; long before the ingredients had Latin names.

She liked the history in the wall of precise, square drawers. Pharmacists had kept drugs in them, and the curing value of those old medicines imparted weight to the power of the substances that now lay inside. This was true, even to those people not seeped in old country ways. The wall of drawers contrasted with the more commercial displays in her shop—a rack of sunglasses, cassettes of country-western singers and rock and roll bands, T-shirts displayed on hooks on the opposite wall, vivid plastic sandals in all styles and colors, and the beaded jewelry she made while she waited for customers.

Rochelle had been born Roberto Manuel Castro Sanchez in Sherman, Texas. Only God and her *Abuela* Angelina knew what had called her Puerto Rican family away from the familiar azure ocean and tropical green of their island home to the dusty middle of the United States, thousands of miles from the Caribbean Sea. When Roberto was ten years old, the meat packing plant where the family worked moved its operations to Kansas. *Abuela* and her extended family followed. The move didn't change things. Rochelle was still Roberto, the skinny, delicate-faced Puerto Rican boy adrift in a sea of children born to brown-skinned Central American workers, and white boys who talked about football and pheasant hunting in loud voices with broad, flat vowels. Roberto felt isolated from the other children. His only friend was Bonnie, a girl with lank hair who still sucked her thumb when she thought no one was watching, and called Roberto, "Sis."

It became worse when Roberto turned fourteen and grew long legs like a colt's and a mane of black hair that hung down his back. His classmates still avoided him, but occasionally he noticed one of the older schoolboys, or their fathers, would look at him, their eyes a little too bright and focused. Angelina, still regal, wise, and the undisputed head of their little band of a family, had seen the looks aimed toward the coltish boy and sent him to live with her son in Miami.

Uncle Martin owned a curio shop that sat in the middle of a narrow street, away from the bright and sparkle of Miami's white beaches. Roberto worked at his uncle's shop after school and on weekends. Martin's wife, Evita, had made Roberto feel welcome in their home alongside the three young grandchildren they were raising. Evita was the first person to call Roberto by the name Rochelle, after Roberto announced one Sunday after dinner that he had been born with the wrong parts, had always known he was female, and would never again answer to the name Roberto. Martin had been less enthusiastic. Still, he made sure Rochelle finished high school and two years of community college.

Each week, Martin paid Rochelle a small sum to dust and sweep his dark, little shop and, when she was older, to mind the counter. He'd narrow his eyes when Rochelle wobbled into the shop in heeled sandals, a T-shirt tied high to show a span of smooth brown belly above fitted shorts.

"*Mija*," Martin would say cocking an eyebrow, "good thing your grandma Angelina sent you to me. Those cowboys, they would think you're pretty after being out all summer with their sheep."

"Cows, Uncle," Rochelle said, rolling her eyes at Martin. "They have cows in Kansas, not sheep."

"Cows, sheep, whatever. Those cowboys would tip their hats to you when you walked by and grin, then you'd be turned around and running back down the street twisting your ankles this way and that in those shoes."

Rochelle saw the reality in what Martin said and was again grateful for Angelina's wisdom in sending her to Martin, to Miami.

Working at the shop had saved her too. She was fascinated looking at the twisted and fragrant clumps sitting on shelves, in boxes or in amber and blue glass bottles. Even more fascinating were the things she found floating in jars behind the curtain that separated her uncle's shop from his private space. There were flaking, coiled snakes, dried scorpions, and roots that looked like twisted human figures lying in the bottoms of bottles of high potency alcohol.

Occasionally, her uncle shooed Rochelle to the front of the store and guided a customer behind the curtain. She would hear voices murmur and the soft sounds of bottle tops being unscrewed. She'd sneak behind the curtain after the customer left, the sharp scent of alcohol, along with things pungent and earthy, floating in the air, secret and mysterious. Rochelle learned much from Martin, how he watchfully listened to customers, drawing them out and asking them questions about their families or their love life or the troubles they had with neighbors. Each question Martin asked spiraled them closer to their weaknesses and longings, even longings they hadn't yet recognized.

Rochelle dabbed the tissue between her breasts again. A shimmer of movement in the hot street outside the shop caught her eye. She watched three teenagers walk down the street. Their skinny arms and narrow boy hips contrasted with their wide shoulders. It was their arms and the chin fuzz they carefully tended that gave away their youth. These boys with their unearned swagger and baggy pants were interesting to watch, but they didn't excite her like they had twenty years ago.

The boys' heads turned in unison to stare at Rochelle's shop and it was then that she noticed the epicanthic folds of their eyes and the narrow chins. They were Vietnamese, or maybe, Cambodian. There was something about their practiced saunter and steely eyes that worried Rochelle. She moved to stand in front of the window so the boys could see her, to let them know they were being watched.

She sold potions to many Vietnamese and Cambodian customers, as well as to residents of this Hispanic neighborhood. The city had worked hard to assimilate the diverse cultures that had arrived to work in the processing plants. But old biases, and competition for jobs and housing, simmered beneath the surface. The discontentment between the different cultures was more vocalized in the pockets of their ethnic neighborhoods, where the veil of tolerance slipped.

The prejudices of the diverse groups were magnified by gangs of boys who competed for the drug trade market, as well as for the difficult but high paying, processing plant jobs. What worried Rochelle was the attitude of this group of boys with their defiant walk through her neighborhood. That and the way their hands occasionally wandered to the pockets of the pants they wore low on their hips. She was so intent on watching them that the bell startled her when the shop door opened.

A woman entered, her walk stiff and halting. She wore a long-sleeved, cotton blouse, even though the thermometer on the bank down the street read 103 degrees. Rochelle arched her brows as she examined the woman, from her uncombed hair to the scuffed athletic shoes.

"Hello, Valerie," said Rochelle. "How have you been?"

"Okay, I guess," Valerie mumbled, refusing to look at Rochelle.

"I haven't seen you for a couple weeks," Rochelle said lightly as she studied Valerie's face and the dark glasses that remained perched on her nose.

"Been busy," Valerie mumbled, still not meeting Rochelle's eyes.

"Valerie? Look at me."

The woman turned slowly, her face cast down.

"Girlfriend, take those glasses off. Let me look at you."

Valerie slowly pulled her sunglasses down. Her left eye was swollen almost shut. A green and blue bruise spread from brow to cheekbone. The bruises were a vivid contrast to her pale skin.

"Let me guess," Rochelle said, "you and Tran went a round again? And you lost?"

"It doesn't hurt much," Valerie said, a tear shimmering and then squeezing out between the puffy lids of her eye.

"A day or so ago, I suspect."

Valerie shrugged her shoulders but said nothing.

"Come here." Rochelle pointed to a bar stool beside the glass-topped counter. "Sit down. I've got something to take the red out of that eyeball. It'll reduce the swelling so you can see better."

"Let's see," Rochelle said walking to the bank of drawers. She pulled open one. A minty scent waffled out and Rochelle pinched two dried leaves off a stem. She opened another drawer and broke off a piece of cinnamon-colored bark. Rochelle added the ingredients to a stone mortar bowl and then went back to the drawers again, this time pulling out a dried twist of root. She crumbed it into the mortar with the rest. Rochelle shot a look at Valerie out of the corner of her eye, making sure Valerie was watching her work. Then she picked up the pestle and ground the ingredients together, adding water until it was a thick paste.

"Yes, that'll work good." She looked up at the woman who, during the time it took Rochelle to prepare the paste, had lifted her chin. Valerie caught Rochelle looking at her and she lowered her eyes again, drawing herself into what Rochelle thought looked like a frightened hedgehog.

"Hop up here on the stool and let me spread this around your eye. We'll let it sit for a while so it has time to bring the swelling down. Close your eyes now." Rochelle cupped Valerie's chin with one hand and used the other to scoop and spread the paste around Valerie's eye and over the bruised cheekbone, all the while humming softly.

"Val, honey, didn't I give you a pamphlet a couple of months ago? The one from the battered women's shelter?"

Valerie lifted a shoulder.

"Was that a yes or a no, girl?"

"Yes," Valerie mumbled. "I read a little of it. Then Tran came home. He doesn't like me reading."

"Tran doesn't like a lot of things. Or, maybe, it's things he likes too much? Like his supper ready on the table when he walks in the door, no matter the time. Or, maybe, he likes too much his shirts pressed just so. You think that's possible?"

"Maybe," Valerie said, giving the same one shoulder shrug.

"Let me get a wet cloth to put over your eye. Keep it moist. Stay here for a minute and don't open that eye or it'll sting." Rochelle walked to the sink beside the soda machine and ran water until it was cool. She brought the wet towel to Valerie and placed it gently over her eye. "Hold this on your eye for a few minutes," she said. She scrapped the rest of the paste into a plastic bag, again humming softly.

"It's getting worse, isn't it?" Rochelle finally said.

"My eye? No."

"That's not what I mean."

"Maybe," said Valerie, both eyes closed now.

"It always does. One of these days Tran'll go too far and you'll end up in the hospital or worse. You realize that. Don't you?"

"He said he wouldn't do it again, that he loves me."

"He said that to you last time, remember?"

Another shrug, but Rochelle saw an almost imperceptible nod of Valerie's head.

"Sometimes the ones we love say they love us too, but their actions say something different."

"Tran tries. I know he loves me, but it's hard for him. He was the last of his mom's kids, raised in one of those relocation camps. She still cleans motel rooms, did you know that? His mom's sixty-eight now and all worn out from having kids that died, and the hardship of war. She lives with us—you knew that—but she won't even try to speak English at home. I have my girls too. Where would we go?"

"Your parents. Are they around?"

"My parents, yeah, right."

Valerie leaned her forehead against her hand, elbow supported by the counter, as if her head had suddenly become too heavy for her neck to support. Rochelle heard a sob.

"Let me wash your face, honey and see how the poultice is doing. Then we can talk more." Rochelle went back to the sink and filled a plastic bowl with warm water. She was carrying it back when she noticed the same group of Vietnamese boys, again on the sidewalk in front of her store. This time, instead of the languid movements they had exhibited earlier, their hands and arms moved rapidly, with bold gestures. Fingers flashed gang signs. Rochelle looked to where they were gesturing and saw Antonio and his little sister come out the door of the community center. Antonio was holding Marcela's hand, and he was intently watching her as they walked, and she talked. Antonio must have heard something because suddenly he looked up.

"Ah, shit," Rochelle said, as the boys began shouting at each other. Hands went to the pockets of jeans and Rochelle saw pistols emerge.

"Valerie," she screamed, "get down. Now!"

Rochelle threw herself on the floor, skirt catching under her knees as she crawled toward Valerie sitting frozen on the stool. Rochelle pulled Valerie to the floor, as pops of semi-automatic gunfire began in the street.

A pane of window glass, the one with the pellet chip, shattered. Rochelle held Valerie tight as shards of the heavy glass window fell, smashing loudly onto the shop floor.

3

Curtis

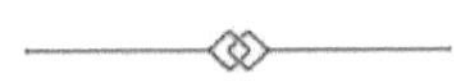

The echo of Alicia's scream was still bouncing off the walls of the reception area when she rounded the desk toward the front door. Curtis stood paralyzed in the doorway of his office, one hand still on the doorknob. He tried to call to Alicia, tell her to wait. Explain it might be dangerous to go outside, but all that came out was a stuttering, "Wa-wa-wa-wait."

It was too late, anyway. Alicia had already pushed through the glass door and Curtis heard her cry out, "Oh God, oh God, no, no," before the door swung shut. Curtis remained frozen. Finally, his legs thawed, and he could move again. Shaking, he picked up the phone sitting on Alicia's desk and punched in 9-1-1.

"Kingston 911," the operator said. "What is your emergency?"

"I think I heard shots outside."

"What is your location?"

"Oh sorry, the community center on east Abilene Street. The address is…." Curtis couldn't recall the address.

"The Kingston Community Youth Center?" asked the operator. "At 9th and East Abilene Streets, is that right?

"Yes."

"You said you heard shots. Was anyone hurt?"

"I don't know," said Curtis. "I can't see anything from here."

There was a brief silence on the line. In the background, Curtis heard keys click and the sound of muted voices.

"You said you heard shots, correct? Police are on their way. Do you need medical assistance?"

Alicia pushed the door open. "Call 911," she shouted, before running back.

Curtis saw blood on the front of her shirt.

"Sir, sir?" asked the operator.

"Yes, better send the medics."

Curtis wanted, he needed, to go outside, find out what happened, but his feet were glued to the floor, unable to take that first step forward. After a time, although he couldn't guess how much time, he pushed open the heavy door of the club and stepped outside. Ten feet away, Antonio sat on the sidewalk, his back to the building, an impossible quantity of blood pooling around him. He was rocking back and forth, arms tight around the limp form of his sister. His face was buried in her dark hair. The movements of his rocking made the girl's braids sway. It was the swaying braids, and the clack of pink and yellow beads on the ends of those braids, that caused Curtis to walk back inside and throw up in Alicia's trash can.

Later, he leaned against the building, in the shadow of the overhang, and watched. The police had arrived first, then the medics and last a woman from the medical examiner's office. It was hot, and Curtis longed for a cold drink of water, but the circle of emergency personnel and stretchers blocked entrance to the club.

"We need to take you to the hospital," a medic said to Antonio. "Looks like you've been shot too. Come on."

Antonio hugged the girl tighter, rocking and saying into her hair, "Oh, *mija*, sorry, so sorry." Sobs came from deep inside him.

Two police officers moved into the circle of emergency workers. One officer spoke sharply, "Antonio, let her go. They need to take you to the hospital. Can't figure out if you're hurt with all this," his hand swept the pool of blood. "Come on."

The other officer stepped in, carefully avoiding the spreading blood, and grabbed Antonio's arm. Antonio shook him off.

"Fuck off. Leave us alone."

"Hey, buddy. Let's go," the second officer said. "We'll get you to the hospital, have them check you out, and then we have questions for you. Come on, now."

Another black and white police car drove up. Curtis watched the officer get out. The man was tall, the short-sleeved uniform shirt tight over muscular arms and thick shoulders. A tattoo, something primitive with thick curved lines, snaked around a bicep and down his forearm. He had buzzed blond hair. When he came closer, Curtis saw the blond hair was shot through with silver. Tanned scalp showed under the clipped hair.

"Hey, Sarge," said the officer still trying to tug Antonio away from his sister. "Come on, Antonio, we haven't got all day. Let them take her so we can figure out what happened here. You know who did this." The last was more a declaration than a question.

The man they called Sarge, Curtis recognized the stripes on his sleeve, patted the officer's back.

"I'll do it," the sergeant said. He squatted beside Antonio, carefully avoiding the blood. Putting a hand on Antonio's shoulder, he spoke softly to him. Curtis couldn't hear what the sergeant said, but after a minute he saw Antonio's head nod once. He kissed Marcela on the forehead, smoothed back her hair, and then looked up at the medical examiner. The sergeant nodded an affirmation to the examiner and Antonio stood. It was only when he bent and clutched his side that Curtis saw the seep of blood from Antonio's abdomen.

Curtis continued to watch as the ambulance left with Antonio and later, after the crime scene techs finished snapping their photographs, watched the coroner bundle the girl's body into a bag, load her into a van, and drive away.

"You're the club director?" someone asked. Curtis jumped. He turned to find the sergeant who had earlier talked to Antonio.

Curtis nodded.

"Let's talk," the officer said. He pointed to the patrol car.

He and the sergeant, Sgt. Nicholas his nametag read, sat in the officer's car. Chilled air blew from dashboard vents. Curtis was glad to be out of the heat.

The sergeant had walked beside Curtis to the patrol car, but didn't say anything more after his question about Curtis' position at the center. Curtis fidgeted, waited for the officer to speak. Finally, he couldn't stand the silence.

"I'm acting as director until Dr. Kline returns. He's been sick."

"Uhmm," said Sgt. Nicholas, writing on a paper attached to a clipboard. Occasionally, a voice sounded from the police radio, but the sergeant ignored it.

"Do you know what happened?" Curtis asked. "I was inside."

"You heard the shots, right? That's when you made the 911 call?"

"Yes. Do you think it was gang related? The damn gangs are taking over the neighborhoods. I heard Antonio was the leader of one."

"You didn't see what was happening outside, before the shooting?"

asked the officer, ignoring Curtis' question.

"No, I was in my office. It doesn't have any windows."

Sergeant Nicholas looked at him. One side of his mouth lifted in a lopsided smile. The skin around his blue eyes crinkled for a brief moment, like what Curtis said amused him.

"You're not in Director Kline's office with the window?" Nicholas asked.

"No."

"Tell me what you know about Marcela's day before the shooting."

Curtis told him, shading his answer to leave out how rushed he had been to finish the application and how annoyed he was by the girl's interruption.

"Alicia, your assistant, said the victim was upset about something. That true?"

Curtis saw the story he had so carefully crafted begin to lean like a house of cards. The sergeant had poked through the veneer of his accounting and learned what Curtis had tried to hide.

"I had to get a grant application done today so we can get funding to continue operations. Government money is tight, you know." He tried to deflect the intense look Nicholas gave him. "The problem, you know, is gang violence—Mexican on Vietnamese, Mexican on Mexican, Vietnamese against Laotian. That's what you should be focusing on."

The officer stared at Curtis and something he couldn't fathom flickered behind the ice eyes. "You think we should just let them duke it out, eventually eliminate the problem?" he said.

"Maybe," said Curtis. "Except for this." He waved his hand at the scene outside the car window.

"Yeah, except for that." The sergeant looked hard at Curtis then turned back to write on the clipboard.

"It's the drug trade, that's the problem," said Curtis, wanting, needing, to fill the uncomfortable silence. "It's gangs and it's the drugs they bring in."

"Yep, it's the sellers." Sergeant Nicholas paused. "And it's the buyers. Wouldn't have the sellers if we didn't have buyers, and that market crosses all cultural lines. And don't forget, alcohol can be abused too."

He gave Curtis a long look and Curtis wondered how much this officer knew of his history. He felt a tentacle of hot embarrassment creep up his spine. He thought about the dark days and nights after the layoff and divorce, and how the warm tingle of a drink drifting down his throat filled the hollow space in his heart. At least it did until the night in the bar with the fight and his arrest.

"Our economy's been bad since the beef packing plant shifted part of their operations to the new plant in Nebraska," said Sgt. Nicholas. "The packers come in, take advantage of tax incentives and cheap labor. Then the equipment wears out and the incentives stop. They move on and what's left? People out of place and out of jobs." He shrugged thick shoulders and watched the activity on the other side of the windshield. A fire truck had arrived and was washing blood off the sidewalk. The water, tinted rust, streamed along the curb until it reached a storm drain and disappeared.

Curtis leaned his head against the backrest. It had been an exhausting day. He and Nicholas talked a little more and Curtis tried to figure him out. With his muscular build and piercing eyes, Curtis figured he'd bring the force of the law on the gangs and drug trade. Instead, it seemed like the cop alternated between mocking Curtis' view of the mostly-Hispanic neighborhood and nudging him toward something he couldn't understand. The sergeant asked Curtis what he did at the community center but his answer—that he oversaw club operations and reported to the board— didn't appear to satisfy the man's question.

The sun was low by the time Curtis pulled into the parking stall in front of his apartment. He turned off the motor and reached for his briefcase. Then he remembered the grant application.

"Ah, shit," he said, pounding the steering wheel. "Shit, shit, shit."

Where had he left it? He'd been on his way out, then there were the shots, and he made the 911 call. Had Alicia left it on the receptionist's desk in her rush out the door? Curtis started the engine and backed out of the parking stall. If he went back for the application tonight, he could mail it on his way to work tomorrow. It would be late, but if he explained what happened, perhaps they would still consider it.

Afterwards, Curtis sat for a while in his car at the club's parking lot. A manila envelope with the application tucked inside was on the passenger seat beside him. The stupid, damn grant application. That had been the start of this entire problem. He just had to get it in the mail before the last pick up, no matter what. He'd found the papers scattered on the floor under the receptionist's desk.

Guilt suffocated him, like the heat inside the car. If he hadn't rushed the girl from his office, would this have happened? Was he complicit in her death or was it simply a consequence of Antonio's gang affiliation, something over which Curtis had no control and no responsibility? He remembered the cop asking him what his job was at the club and the odd way the sergeant responded when he answered.

Movement across the street caught his eye. Sergeant Nicholas, now in civilian clothes, was helping a woman cover a broken storefront window with a plywood panel. The woman was striking, with warm brown skin and straight black hair that fell nearly to her waist. She wore shorts, revealing long, tan legs. A sleeveless shirt, tied at her waist, pulled taunt across her breasts when she lifted her arms to hold the plywood in place. She and Nicholas moved in an easy coordination and, although Curtis couldn't hear what they were saying, he could see they talked as they worked. He watched for a few minutes, then started the car and drove out of the lot.

At home, Curtis fixed a sandwich and poured a glass of Coke. He sat them on the table beside the chair, leaned his head back against the recliner and closed his eyes. He was tired and his limbs felt heavy. The ten o'clock news had begun, and the weather reporter was broadcasting a quick, top of the hour, summary of tomorrow's forecast.

Curtis startled when the phone rang, the noise jerking him back from the edge of sleep.

"Curtis?" the caller asked.

"Amy?" His ex-wife's voice sounded strained.

"I saw on the news what happened. Thought I would, well, you know, Melody was worried."

"I'm okay," Curtis said.

"Oh. Well, that's good to hear."

Her words were awkward, but her tone had softened, and Curtis fantasized for a minute that she would ask more about how he was doing, like she had done when she cared about him—before bitterness ate at their marriage. The glimmer of hope winked out with her next words.

"Melody wants to talk to you. She wants to make sure you're okay."

Curtis heard rustling as the phone changed hands.

"Hi, Daddy," Melody said in the familiar, flat voice he loved. He closed his eyes and could picture her; head tilted, like always, toward the phone's handset, intent on catching every word the caller spoke. "I saw you on the news. Who was the girl that was killed?"

Her question caused a cascade of images: the uncertainty in Marcela's eyes as she exited his office, her quick smile when Alicia praised her work, the clack of beads, blood congealing on the sidewalk.

"Dad? Are you still there?"

"She was a girl from the community center's daycare. Marcela was her name." His throat tightened and the name came out raspy.

"How old was she?"

"Six or seven, I think," said Curtis.

"Oh, I'm almost ten," said Melody and deftly changed subjects. "Did I tell you about my report card? I got a B in math. It's my hardest class. The rest I got all As."

"Good for you. I always knew you were the smart one in the family."

Again, she deftly switched topics.

"Are you still picking me up Saturday?"

"Sure, I'll be there around nine, like always," said Curtis.

"Okay. Bye, Dad." She paused, said in a softer voice, "I love you, Daddy."

"Love you, too, baby. See you Saturday."

Curtis placed the phone back in its receiver and went to the kitchen. He opened the Glenlivit bottle, then paused and screwed the lid back on. He ran water in the glass, added ice and sat back down. The ten o'clock news was still on, but he kept the volume muted as he watched scenes play across the screen.

Curtis sipped the water and balanced the glass on the fat arm of the recliner. He closed his eyes, letting his head rest against the cushion. Images replayed in his mind: the bright star sticker on Marcela's paper; police urging the crowd to disburse; two old Mexican ladies holding each other, one crying and twisting a rosary through her fingers; yellow crime scene tape strung across the front of the club; glass shards from the broken store window across the street glittering on the sidewalk; Sergeant Nicholas; Antonio holding his sister's body.

Marcela's motionless body morphed, and Antonio was holding a girl with light brown, curly hair. The girl's legs stretched beyond Antonio's lap. Her feet lay the same way Melody's always did, one foot pointed up and the other foot pointed in. Antonio shifted and Curtis recognized his daughter's face. He jerked when he saw her. From far away, he heard glass shatter. Heart racing Curtis woke, the flickering television screen replacing the vision of Melody lying bloody and still in Antonio's arms.

4

Rochelle

———◇———

Twice, Rochelle swept the shop floor in front of the broken window, but slender shards of glass hid in the gaps between the boards of the old, white pine floor. She had put away the broom and dustpan in the storage room and walked back only to see sunlight glitter on a piece of glass she missed. This time when she walked back, she deliberately looked out the unbroken window instead of at the floor.

Sometime, in the pre-dawn hours, bundles of flowers, still in their transparent cellophane wrappers, and a forlorn stuffed bear had appeared, propped against the side of the community center where Marcela had died.

Rochelle lived in an apartment above her shop. Earlier, while her coffee brewed, she watched the old priest from St. Guadalupe's Church place a white cross in the middle of the makeshift memorial and then stand for a few minutes, his head bowed. Throughout the morning, the sad collection had grown as people added more flower bouquets, stuffed animals, and votive candles in tall glass vessels imprinted with images of Jesus, lambs, and the Virgin Mary.

Rochelle opened a drawer behind one of the shop's counters. She poured round beads of green jade out of an envelope and into a shallow dish. Another envelope held larger, silver filigreed beads and she shook a few of them out and added them to the dish. Then she picked up a large blunt needle and threaded elastic string through the needle's large eye. She first pushed the needle through a piece of cork to close off one end of the string and then dipped it into the pan of beads, stringing four jade beads for every silver one. When she noticed movement in the street, she'd stop and watch as people slowly walked over to examine the collection or add something new. It was hot outside and even though the front of the community center building was in the shade in the morning, the flowers quickly drooped. Once, Alicia, the center's receptionist, brought out a plastic bowl of ice and slipped pieces of ice inside the cellophane wrappers. Rochelle didn't think the ice would hold off the flowers' decline very long but understood the reasoning behind Alica's attempt to slow the decay.

The door of the community center opened around noon. A man stepped out and looked at the collection, his back to the street. Rochelle had seen him before but had not met him. Customers told her he was appointed by the center's board of directors as interim director while Mark Kline recovered from his illness. One of her customers mentioned the interim director's name; Curtis, she recalled. She rarely saw him, just glimpses during the week as he walked from his car in the parking lot beside the community center to a side door reserved for staff. His knit shirt and khaki pants were rumpled, and his shoulders were slumped. She could see a film of sweat on the top of his bald head.

A motorcycle engine started down the street and the man jumped at the sound. She watched, still holding the necklace she'd been stringing. Then, she put the bead work down, slid off the chair and went to meet him.

"It's a nice memorial for Marcela," said Rochelle.

Curtis startled and turned to face her. His eyes were red, and his round face flushed like he had been working hard to hold back tears.

"Oh. Yes," said Curtis.

Rochelle waited to see if the man would say more but he didn't, just turned back to stare at the collection. Even in the shade the air was hot, and no breeze offered comfort. The synthetic fur on the collection of stuffed animals looked bedraggled, as if the stuffed bears and kittens longed for the cool interior of the stores where they had been purchased.

"Is the community center going to sponsor a memorial event or something? I know they did in the past when Mark Kline was director. They organized a candlelight vigil a couple of years ago when a boy from the neighborhood was hit by a car and killed."

Curtis faced Rochelle, and she saw the flush had spread down his neck. His reaction surprised her. She wondered if she had earlier misread sorrow in his posture and rumpled clothes. There was something going on with this man, but she wasn't sure yet what it was.

"I am not Director Kline, and, in fact, I doubt he will be back," said Curtis emphasizing the words not and doubt. The man is over seventy and seriously ill. What he has done in the past in this neighborhood does not mean we have to do the same thing now. I'm the interim director. The board and I make the decisions about what the community center will and will not do."

Rochelle was speechless. Curtis wiped his wet forehead with the palm of a trembling hand. Did he feel a responsibility for the girl's death on the doorstep of a place he was supposed to oversee? She had heard from customers that he did not use Mark Kline's office and, although he seemed competent handling administrative duties of the center, they said he didn't demonstrate affection or empathy toward either the staff or the people who used the center. She wondered if the banishment from Kline's office was this man's decision, anticipating Kline's return, or one foisted on him. Rochelle held Curtis' eyes but didn't speak.

"Who did you say you are?" asked Curtis.

His face was still pink, but his expression had changed from anger to one closer to embarrassment.

"I'm Rochelle Castro Sanchez. I own the shop across the street." She gestured behind her at the store. She let her hand drop, not offering it for the man to shake. He didn't seem to notice the affront.

"I see. I'm Curtis Myerson. Do you own the shop, or you just work there?" His tone had softened, and he smiled at her. The smile, however, did not reach his eyes.

"It's my shop."

Something flicked across the man's face, but again Rochelle couldn't decipher his thoughts. Was it curiosity or skepticism that a young Hispanic woman was able to own a business? His gaze moved down to focus on her breasts. Rochelle straightened her shoulders, causing her breasts to thrust forward. She did not intend it to be sexual, but as armament against his rudeness. At five feet, eight inches, she was an inch or so taller than Curtis, but she longed for her two-inch heels and the height advantage it would provide against this strange man. Curtis opened his mouth as if to say something, but before he could speak, she heard her shop door open across the street. The bell above the door tinkled its welcome. Turning, without a word of goodbye to Curtis, she strode away.

Rochelle was surprised to see the customer was Lucia Gomez, Marcela's mother. She looked terrible. Always thin, she seemed to have shrunk even more, shedding height as well as flesh. Black slacks and a worn grey blouse hung loose on her body. Sharp cheekbones stood out in a gaunt face and her eyes were red, the lids swollen. Rochelle took Lucia's hand with both of hers. The limp hand was cool, and the bones felt fragile under Rochelle's fingers.

"I am very sorry for your loss," said Rochelle. She switched to Spanish, "*¿Por favor, que puedo hacer para ayudarte?*" What can I do to help? Rochelle felt Lucia tremble and she pulled away her hand. She turned from Rochelle, dug through her purse, pulled out a crumbled tissue and wiped her eyes. When she faced Rochelle, her eyes were dry, and her mouth set in a tight line.

"The police said you saw what happened, but he wouldn't tell me much. I need to know what happened to my baby." Lucia's voice was shaky. The words were determined.

Rochelle opened her mouth to speak, hesitated. What could she say to this mother that wouldn't become a sharp blade to further injure her? She suspected the police officer Lucia referred to was Jim Nicholas and that he was the one who told Lucia she was a witness. Damn him for pawning off this chore on her.

How could she, who could never birth a child and, so, would never see one die a senseless death, offer comfort to this mother? She would have to shape what happened to provide details, but not the horrible truth of a scene that would forever haunt Lucia in the early morning hours when the rest of the world slept. What were the words that could fill the spaces in this mother's heart with the details of what happened, but not increase her pain? She needed time to think.

"Lucia, would you like some iced tea? It's so hot outside today. Maybe, some iced tea with sugar and mint to refresh us? Please sit. It will take me only a minute."

Rochelle poured sweet tea into tall glasses of ice. She had made it earlier, setting a glass jar with tea bags on the small balcony off her upstairs apartment. It didn't take long for the summer heat and sun to transform the water from clear to a rich brown. She rolled fresh mint leaves between her fingers to release their crisp scent, placed them atop the ice, and carried the glasses to where Lucia sat. She could see the woman's tension in her stiff posture—as unyielding as the metal chair on which she sat.

While she had prepared their tea, Rochelle reviewed the scene from yesterday: the cocky walk of the Asian boys, the door of the community center opening, Antonio intent on listening as Marcela spoke. Then the shouts, flash of gang signs, gunshots, the smell of cordite, and so much blood on the sidewalk.

Rochelle sat the glasses down, took a seat beside Lucia, and watched her take a drink. Lucia's hand trembled as she lifted the glass to her mouth.

"Antonio and Marcela were talking when they came out," Rochelle began. "They didn't see the boys across the street at first."

"Antonio wouldn't have come out if he knew they were there," said Lucia, both a declaration and a question in the statement.

"Yes, I know he wouldn't have put Marcela in danger if he knew. The boys started shouting at each other and it went bad from there. Sgt. Nicholas told you the rest?"

"Some. He said it was quick, Marcela wouldn't have had a chance to be afraid or to feel hurt."

Rochelle hoped it was true. She had been crawling across the floor to pull Valerie down and didn't see whether Marcela struggled or had been stilled with the first shot. What Jim told Lucia was true enough for this telling. "Yes, I believe that is true."

Lucia drew in a deep breath and let it out slowly. A tear ran down one cheek.

"That's good," Lucia said. "I didn't want her to suffer."

"She didn't suffer," Rochelle agreed.

"Those boys who shot my baby. They were Vietnamese from the Dragon Boyz gang?"

"Is that what the police told you or what Antonio told you?"

Lucia covered her eyes with the crumpled tissue, wiped away the tears. When she lowered the tissue and looked at Rochelle, fury had replaced her sorrow. It was if the tears, now captured in the damp tissue, contained her grief, instead of tears being a manifestation of the emotion.

"Their evil has destroyed my family. I'm not going to let them come into my neighborhood and think they can get away with murdering my baby." Lucia lifted her chin and glared at Rochelle. A steely defiance had been added to the grief in her dark eyes.

Rochelle stirred her tea, searched for words that would calm the woman. What did Lucia have in mind? The tensions between the Asians and Hispanics had been building for a long time. They competed for jobs at the packing plant, they competed for homes made expensive by the scarcity of inexpensive housing in a city that hadn't been ready to accommodate the influx of workers, and they competed for the right to weave their cultural traditions into the torn fabric of the community. Besides, did her opinion even have legitimacy? She was Puerto Rican in a city of whites, Asians, and Central America Hispanics. And she was female in a body born male.

"Lucia, please," Rochelle pleaded. She reached for Lucia's hand and held it between both of hers. "I know you're angry and hurt. I am, too, at what has happened, but escalating the problem with revenge isn't going to make you feel better."

Lucia jerked her hand back and stood up. "Easy for you to say. Do you have kids? No. Will you ever feel this pain? I know you can never. I know what you are. You can't know the pain of losing a child. It's three for me. I lost three babies, now. How you say you know what a mother feels. How can any man know, just 'cause you put on a dress."

"That's not fair, Lucia, and you know it." Rochelle sat, unmoving, in her chair. The old alienation of her childhood raised its ugly head from deep inside her, from a place where she thought she had buried it.

"I gotta go plan a funeral for my Marcela," said Lucia. When she yanked the shop door open, the abrupt action caused the bell above the door to clang rudely.

Rochelle looked around at the beautiful oak pharmacy bins against one wall. Their contents offered reprieve to customers who sought a link with their past, but now Rochelle imagined the reprieve as no more than a vague pittance. To Rochelle, the drawer's contents represented her life purpose as well as a livelihood in this dusty town. Perhaps, the only value the old bins held with their tarnished brass pulls were merely a connection to her happier life in Miami with Uncle Martin's family?

She looked at the other side of the store with its collection of CDs, sunglasses, and clothing. This shop was her creation, what she had believed could offer her a living: holistic medicine for some customers and commercial wears for others. But were the contents actually a reflection of her? Half of the shop held a shaman's tools—a balm to believers. The other half offered cheap trinkets, clothing, shoes, and costume jewelry. Did she simply conjure up an illusion of a businesswoman that veiled the truth of who she really was? What was that truth? Was Rochelle a shopkeeper who worked as a shaman or was this a façade like the mix-up in her brain wiring that insisted she was a different gender than the one she had been born?

Rochelle gazed out the window at Marcela's memorial. The white cross the priest had left early in the morning had tilted, one arm sinking toward the pavement. The flowers were wilted and most of the votive candles had winked out, the hot sun melting the candle wax and drowning the flame.

Rochelle recalled her *Abuela* Angelina's funeral. The old woman's heart had finally given up, but the mourners at Angelina's wake and funeral had been able to reminisce on her long life—birth and childhood in Puerto Rico, children and grandchildren, dreams realized, and hopes that had borne fruit. The long fade to her death had given friends and family an opportunity to say goodbye, to make amends for old grudges, retell old stories, and thank her for past favors. For Rochelle, it had been a time to thank the old woman for saving her.

Not so with Marcela. The time needed to fulfill her dreams, or even to fashion a dream for her future, had been stolen from her. Even the time to tell her goodbyes had been stolen. At Marcela's funeral there would be no speeches about her accomplishments. There had been no opportunity for family and friends to say farewell to the living Marcela.

Rochelle saw the door of the center open, and Curtis step out. He looked at the display of flowers and then across the street at Rochelle's shop. He stood for a moment on the curb, rocking back and forth on his feet as if trying to decide. Then, he stepped off the curb and walked across the street toward Rochelle's shop.

5

Curtis

————◇————

Time marched grimly toward noon. At least that's what the morning after the girl's death felt like to Curtis. Alicia sat at the receptionist's desk and, like any other day, she greeted each parent as they arrived to drop off their children at the day care. This morning, Curtis didn't hear the usual, high-spirited conversations. Alicia usually bounced here and there with an energy he found tiresome. Today, she moved through the morning in a thick fog, unsure what objects lay hidden on the path.

Curtis spent the morning reconciling the center's bank statement. He enjoyed the task, tallying the deposits and withdrawals. There was always a moment of suspense when he joined the totals—subtracted the withdrawals from the deposits to see if they matched the balance on the bank statement. He especially enjoyed the months when the balance he calculated was different than the bank's balance. First, he'd check his math. If it was correct, he'd examine each check and compare the amount written to what was reported on the bank statement. One time, he discovered the bank had made an eleven-cent mistake, transposing two numbers on the check for an electric bill.

Curtis called the bank. He enjoyed pointing out their mistake. The bank even sent him a letter acknowledging their mistake and thanking him for the center's continued business. He still had the letter in his drawer, tucked away in its envelope, under a box of paper clips. Today, even though his reconciliation matched exactly with that of the bank, the satisfaction the task usually provided was muted.

Alicia was still at the receptionist's desk; staying far away from him, Curtis suspected. She had already been on the phone when came into the building and didn't acknowledge his arrival. That was fine with him. The day was difficult enough without having to deal with her accusatory looks. Curtis glanced at the clock. It was 10:18 and Alicia was still on the phone. It had rung insistently since he arrived, but he had been busy with the bank statement and didn't pay attention to her conversations. The phone rang again, and this time he listened.

"No, we don't have anything planned yet."

There was a long pause while Alicia listened to the caller and then she said, "Yes, that would be a good idea."

Silence as she listened. "No, I don't know. They said they'd announce the place and time of the funeral later. I'm sure it'll be in the newspaper."

He heard the cordless handset rattle as Alicia placed the phone back in its cradle. Immediately, it rang again. Alicia picked it up. She said, "Hello," and then switched to Spanish.

Curtis turned to the folders in his in-box. The part-time receptionist came in at 11:30. Maybe then, Alicia would help him with the work rather than chatting on the damn phone. He opened the top folder. It contained the agenda draft for the youth center's next board meeting. Curtis was still proof reading it when he heard Alicia talking to Roberta, the part-time receptionist. He heard footsteps and Alicia appeared.

"Curtis?" she said, standing in front of his desk.

"Yes," he said, trying not to act annoyed. He disliked the informality of Alicia using his first name. More than once, he had instructed her to call him Mr. Myerson, but despite the reminders, she again dropped the informality of his first name into the room like an insult.

"I've had several calls asking if we're planning a vigil or something for Marcela," Alicia began. "A candlelight vigil would be nice. We could invite the mayor or someone like that."

Now she was on a roll.

"Or we could have it in the park down the street and follow the vigil up with a picnic for anyone who wants to stay."

Alicia stopped talking, looking expectantly at Curtis.

"I'm sure they'll have a memorial service for her. But that kind of planning is up to Marcela's family, not us. Our job is to keep on doing what we've been doing."

Curtis opened a desk drawer and took out a fresh pen hoping Alicia would get the hint that she had been dismissed. She didn't.

"A vigil is different than a memorial. The funeral service is for family and friends, to honor the dead. A vigil is something to bring the neighborhood together, bring awareness to the violence problem. We could even invite representatives from the Vietnamese community. Make it more inclusive than just our neighborhood."

"I don't know if the board will…" Curtis started to say.

Alicia threw up her arms. "This isn't something that the center board and sponsors decide, that would take forever. A vigil is just us, stepping up to recognize a problem."

"Well, I don't know."

Alicia rolled her eyes.

"Think about it. We've had a ton of calls asking. Just make a decision so I can let everyone know. If we don't step up, someone else will need to."

Alicia walked out of the office, heels clicking determinedly on the linoleum floor.

Curtis turned back to the folders in his box. He couldn't understand this rehashing of a painful event. It was much better to move on, to get life back to normal as quickly as possible. Dredging up the girl's death—and his actions preceding it—was like the Monday morning analysis of a big Sunday football game. One could carefully analyze each incomplete pass, each failed end-run, but no matter how one reshuffled the game to change the outcome, yesterday's game was just that—past, over, and done.

After all, he had lain awake in bed in the predawn hours and done just that. If he had talked more to the girl, would it have delayed her leaving the center, the window of time for the shooting closing before they ventured outside? If Antonio hadn't been listening so closely to Marcela's recitation of her day, would he have seen the shooters and recognized the danger before he pushed the door open? Minute by minute, Curtis had analyzed the afternoon, trying to determine what little change in the timeline of events would have altered the outcome. Even before he got in his car to drive to work, he knew all the scrutiny of the prior day's events, his fervent prayer to alter one link in the chain that led to the girl's death, had changed nothing.

Now, he was being asked to relive it, not in his private space in the sacred hours before dawn where one might believe that hope and prayer could change fate. No, he was being asked to try and amend fate in a public way, in front of a community where, yes, admit it, he had no expectation that he could change the neighborhood's perspective. A vigil wouldn't calm the neighborhood. It would simply spark anger and drive a wider wedge between the Hispanics and the Vietnamese.

He couldn't understand why they weren't able to get along. They were both minorities in this town and they struggled with the same problems of poverty and displacement. You'd think each would empathize with the mutual struggles of the other. Or maybe not. If they combined forces, they could become greater than their individual parts. His people—farmers, businessmen, others, who had been here for generations—would become the minority. Curtis wondered how it felt to move to a country where the language and customs were different. Could he adjust? How would it feel to bump against the invisible force field that kept him out of neighborhoods and guided him toward enclaves where the housing was shoddy, and familiar food and traditions unattainable?

Curtis looked at the folder of billing notices, but he had lost his desire to work. Standing, he rolled tense shoulders. If he went outside in the fresh air and away from the nagging ring of the phone, it would give him time to clear his thoughts and decide what to do. He hesitated for a moment, remembering his earlier encounter with the woman from the shop across the street. He had gone to look at the spot on the sidewalk where Marcela died. What had he hoped for? That the previous day was simply a bad dream? The somber tone that greeted him when he entered the center from his usual side door entrance had told him the answer, but still he had to see. Was any of the girl's blood still there, a gory reminder?

He discovered it wasn't blood on the sidewalk that evidenced the previous day's events, but a makeshift memorial with candles in jars, bundles of flowers, and stuffed animals. In the middle of the collection was a picture of Marcela, a school photograph, he figured, with the generic mottled background that always characterized school photos. Marcela was smiling in the photo, her hair softly curling over one shoulder. Curtis shifted position and it seemed Marcela's eyes followed him. There was accusation in the dark depths.

He had jumped when he felt a touch on his arm and his heart lurched when he saw the beautiful woman standing next to him. She was the same one he had seen yesterday boarding up the broken shop window. Her figure was sensual, the tops of her breasts rounded above her low-cut blouse. They talked briefly before Rochelle mentioned Dr. Kline. At mention of yhe old director, Curtis had felt the bumbling inadequacy he had faced ever since he was a child fill his chest, and he'd snapped at the woman. Damn if once again he had stammered and been cross when confronted by someone he wanted to impress.

Most likely, the attractive shopkeeper was gone by now, and he could find a few minutes of peace before he had to come back and face the unpaid bills on his desk. And Alicia's persistent hints about a vigil.

The woman, Rochelle, Curtis now recalled her name, mentioned a vigil too. She wasn't wearing a wedding ring. True, he had seen the police sergeant, Jim Nicholas, helping her board up the window, but there was nothing in their actions that hinted of more than a law enforcement officer working to protect a victim's property. Rochelle was beautiful and Curtis felt a connection when they talked. He could talk to her and get her ideas about planning a vigil. That would get Alicia off his back and, perhaps, be a starting place for something more with Rochelle.

"Be back in a minute," Curtis mumbled to Alicia as he rounded the reception desk toward the Center's door. He didn't wait for a reply.

The collection of flowers and mementos were still there. There was a white cross in the middle that had started to fall, making it look as wilted as the flower bouquets baking inside their cellophane wrappers.

He stood on the sidewalk, facing the street for a few minutes and debated what to do. He'd bring up the idea of a vigil with the shop owner. It would give him a second chance with her and appease Alicia. Reaching a decision, Curtis stepped off the curb and made his way across the street.

"I'd like to apologize for this morning," he told Rochelle. "Yesterday was difficult, you understand. You just caught me unexpected." Curtis smiled, giving the woman an opportunity to see he was sincere.

The first thing he had noticed when he walked in the door was the smell: earthy and herbal. He noticed it before, when Rochelle approached him, but he thought it was a fragrance from her shampoo or a perfumed soap. Now, he realized the smell came from the store. It clung to her, making it difficult to separate her scent from the shop's scent. The building was old. The floor had wide, scuffed planks of yellowed pine. Exposed limestone rock walls separated this space from its neighboring shops. The pressed tin-paneled ceiling was high, and the blades of a suspended fan moved slowly, wafting the air and cooling his skin. Most of the merchandise in the store was the typical touristy stuff—T-shirts, shoes, sundries, jewelry—even though they were far from any tourist hot spot.

What surprised Curtis was the wide wall of drawers along the opposite wall. The drawers started at counter height and reached up at least eight feet. An old-fashioned sliding ladder on a rail, like the ones in old library photographs, rested at one end. He wondered about the history of the building, what had been housed here before.

Rochelle watched him for a moment, then spoke, "I appreciate your apology. Yesterday was stressful on all of us. Poor Marcela, so young. Did you know her well?"

"Ah, yes, I guess you could say so," Curtis said, his throat tight. "She was in our office right before, you know." Curtis couldn't hold the woman's eyes. They pierced him. It seemed she could see what really happened the afternoon before. Curtis looked away, felt himself flush.

"That makes it worse, yes?" Rochelle asked, letting the question dangle in the air.

She crossed her arms under her breasts deepening the cleavage. Curtis wanted to fall into that warm, soft crevice and stay forever.

"Sure," Curtis said. "But the reason I came over is that I want to, well, we," he cleared his throat.

Rochelle watched him, expectant.

"Ah, I was thinking about having a vigil for the girl. I mean, Marcela. I thought we could invite the mayor, have candles and stuff. What do you think?"

Rochelle tapped her lips with the tips of long fingers. She said, "It sounds like a good idea. It would be here in the street?"

To Curtis, it seemed her eyes had softened.

He flashed his best smile. "I thought it would be a good place to start. There's a park a couple of blocks from here. We can walk there, afterwards. The park has more room and we'd be out of the street." Yes, this might work for him. He could tell Rochelle was warming to the idea.

"It'd be a good thing for the neighborhood," Curtis added.

"We could invite representatives from the Vietnamese community," said Rochelle. "Many of their members have lost family to violence, you know, with the war and its aftermath."

Curtis rubbed his chin. He thought it was a bad idea to invite those whose kind was responsible for the girl's death. It could create even more problems. "I don't know about that, but, say, you make some good points. Maybe we can get together sometime to discuss it. Dinner?"

Rochelle's eyes narrowed.

Curtis backpedaled. "Or lunch. It's not difficult for me to get away at noon." Curtis rushed on, unable to stop the clumsy words. "I can pick up burgers or some sandwiches. We could have lunch here or at the Center. The park?" Curtis sensed he was losing her. The last came out as a question, but he didn't want to back away now. Not when he had opened the door to spend some time with this sexy lady.

Curtis felt her look, once again, into his soul. He felt naked. The store was quiet; the only sound a faint swish as the blades of the ceiling fan turned.

"I don't think lunch will work," she finally said, her gaze sliding out the window to the street.

Curtis shuffled his feet, tried to capture her eyes again, but she stayed firm, focused on something outside.

"Okay," he finally said, shrugging. "Well, guess I'd better mosey back to work. Lots of work to do, you know. It requires a lot of effort to keep our community center going."

Rochelle turned to Curtis. She smiled, but the warmth didn't reach her eyes. Curtis thought about saying more, something that would again spark the light he saw earlier in her eyes. He opened his mouth, closed it. "Later," he said, and left. As he crossed the street, he wondered if she was watching.

6

Rochelle

———◇———

Rochelle knew Jim was awake. The lighted display on the nightstand clock showed 2:39 a.m. He'd leave at three in the morning, like he always did. First, he'd roll over and sit on the side of the bed for a few minutes, his back to her. Then he'd slide each leg into his jeans and stand to pull them over his muscular ass. She loved the way the muscles in his back and ass bunched when he stood, then relaxed when he bent to grasp the waistband of his jeans.

The last thing he always did before he left was to come to her side of the bed and kiss her, running his hand over her belly to squeeze Rochelle's soft penis. Sometimes, his hand lingered and she would moan and whisper, "Stay for a while," but Jim always shook his head. "Can't," he would tell her then kiss her again, and leave. After he left, Rochelle would scoot over to where his body warmed the bed, but that only seemed to delay the wave of loneliness.

His routine didn't stop Rochelle from trying on the chance this night would be different. She ran her hand down his arm from the hard shoulder to his hand. It always surprised her that she couldn't feel evidence of the thick tattoo that snaked down his arm. Jim stirred and rolled toward her. She took his hand and squeezed it. He squeezed back. Rochelle propped herself on an elbow.

"Jim," she said.

"Umm."

"Can't you stay just one night?" Rochelle hated the pleading tone in her voice. What happened to the brash person she had been in Miami when she first came out. She had taken men to her bed at midnight and pushed them out the door at dawn. There was always another waiting—a young man enchanted with her smile, the curve of her new breasts, what hid under the short skirt. Or there were the older men, striving to satisfy a need they could never express in their marital bed. In this Kansas town, those kinds of men were scarce. Plus, she was a grown woman now. In October she'd turn forty. What she had here, at this time in her life with Jim, wasn't fleeting lust but something deeper, intimate, replenishing.

"Why not?" she asked.

Jim turned toward her. He wrapped his arms around Rochelle and pulled her against his chest. He stroked her exposed breast.

"You know why," he said softly, his face buried in her hair. "I don't need to explain it to you. I'm happy with what we have. I thought you were too."

Rochelle pulled away, said, "I am happy with you. It's just that I feel, I've felt for a long time, that we're in a holding pattern. It's good, but it's not enough anymore." She understood the reasons why Jim had to conceal their relationship but was it fair that it was always her who made the sacrifice?

"Anymore? It's difficult for me, too, Rochelle. Don't you think I want to stay, wake up and fix you breakfast in the morning, see a movie together. Hell, even acknowledge each other in public. But there's too much of a risk. People who don't know you well don't know your secret. Even some people who know, they accept you. But us together, that's something else. What we have is fine between us, but it would be different if our relationship was out in the open, displayed for the whole town to see. It would come back on you. And, on me. I'd risk my job, my friends. Both our lives would implode."

Rochelle wriggled away and pulled the sheet up to cover her breasts. She felt naked and needed protection against all the blunt talk.

"We could go someplace else. It'd be easy for you to get a job with a police department in another city. Like you said, no one would know."

"Ah, hell, Rochelle. What about my sister and her boys? She needs me to help. God knows her worthless ex-husband is a piss-ass example for them. Sam and Jake are teens now and Michael isn't far behind. I need to be here for them, make sure they finish school and stay out of trouble. After they're grown, we can move somewhere else."

"Oh, right," Rochelle said. "I'm just supposed to stay here, accept the little tidbits you throw to me. Oh yeah, the tidbits you throw between ten and three at night?"

"Well, hell." Jim said. "What do you expect me to do? Huh? I'm trapped too. Can't you see that?"

Rochelle tossed her pillow at Jim and got up. She walked barefoot to the bathroom and locked the door behind her. Just once let him wait for her. She used the toilet and splashed water on her face. She brushed her hair, feeling her way in the dark bathroom. When she came back, she found Jim sitting on the side of the bed, a shirt in his hands. He was staring out the window, the glow from the streetlight illuminating the tension lines between his brows.

Rochelle hesitated for a moment before she said, "I have enough money saved."

Jim turned toward her, his face now in shadow. She couldn't read him.

"Remember, I said I was saving money for the last operation to finish my transition to a complete woman." She went on before Jim had a chance to respond. "There's a clinic I found on the East Coast that does the surgery. I already checked into what I need to do. It's something I've wanted for a long time, to be a whole woman." In a lower voice, she said, "If I do that, then there's no secret needing to be kept."

"But I love you just the way you are," said Jim.

"And that's the problem," said Rochelle. She picked up a pillow from where it had fallen on the floor and threw it at the headboard. Jim sat rigid, his face still in shadow. Rochelle wrapped a thin robe around her and went to the kitchenette. She pulled a bottle from the apartment-size refrigerator and poured wine into a glass. She leaned against the counter sipping and tried not to listen to the sounds Jim made as he finished dressing, tried to hold back the tears. Without saying a word, not even goodbye, Jim left, softly pulling the apartment door shut behind him. The latch snapped home with a sense of finality.

7

Curtis

◇

It was ten minutes before the meeting was to start, and the community center's small gymnasium was packed. They had set up all eighty of the chairs they had in storage, but Curtis figured there were at least fifty other people milling around or leaning against the gym's concrete block walls. The gym was air conditioned, but the AC unit was old and far too small to sufficiently cool the large room. An industrial-size fan blocked one doorway blowing in cooler air from the hallways, but it was still uncomfortably warm.

The heat, however, wasn't what was making Curtis' palms sweat. He sat in one of the chairs beside the podium, facing the crowd. To his left, sat three of the Center's board members: Nadine Powers, Roger Williams, and Dr. Michael Schultz. They looked glum as they surveyed the crowd and Curtis wondered what they were thinking. On the other side of the podium were Sister Clarice and Sister Beatrice from the Catholic charity house. Beside them sat an old Vietnamese man Curtis didn't know. The man was small, a little over five feet, Curtis guessed, and thin. He was the only one in the gymnasium wearing a suit and tie and his straight and firm bearing gave him a dignity that contradicted his frail physical stature. The man had introduced himself to Curtis, but he couldn't recall the name. It had been like other Vietnamese names, syllables crashing against each other like cymbals. Curtis patted the shirt pocket that held the slip of paper with the Vietnamese man's name written on it. He hopped he'd be able to pronounce it when it came time to introduce him.

Curtis checked his watch, 6:57. The meeting was scheduled to start at seven. He wondered how many more people were coming. The gym was filled, with little space left to stand. Latecomers would have to listen from the hall. He wished he could stand out in the cool hall and watch as someone else sweated on the make-shift stage and talked to the audience. Dr. Kline was supposed to have been here to introduce the panel and direct the discussion, but his wife called mid-morning to say his doctor advised against it. Now Curtis was stuck with the task.

Earlier in the day, he had taken his lunch, a legal tablet, and pen into

Dr. Kline's office to compose a speech. It had been the nuns' idea to hold a public meeting to discuss what had happened and propose a vigil for Marcela.

Three days earlier, Curtis found the nuns waiting, alert and patient, in the lobby when he arrived at work ten minutes after nine o'clock. He saw them and gave Alicia a sharp look as he passed the front desk on the way to his office. Alicia followed him into the office and began to talk before Curtis had a chance to put down his briefcase and settle behind the desk.

"Sister Beatrice and Sister Clarice, from the *Casa de la Gente* mission house, are here to talk with you about the vigil," Alicia said. She was wringing her hands, and it made Curtis suspect she had a hand in the nuns' appearance in their lobby.

"They're here, why?" asked Curtis.

"Well, I was talking to the priest at my church after mass a couple of days ago. We talked about Marcela and what happened and, you know, it just slipped out that, maybe, we're going to do a vigil."

Just as he suspected.

"A couple of days ago, before I authorized organizing a vigil, you mean?" This woman irritated Curtis, sometimes. She was always just talking to friends or family or center supporters on the phone. They'd talk and all of a sudden, the center had changes or plans that Curtis had not directed and had little input on. The same thing had happened for the spring community clothing drive. The phone rang, Alicia talked, and soon they had cars parked in the lot with their trucks open and folding tables out, and people walking through the lot picking through donated clothing and used appliances. This time, the phone rang, Alicia talked, and there were nuns in the lobby waiting for him and, he was sure, noticing he was late for work.

"We discussed it earlier, you recall," Alicia said. She had stopped the hand wringing. Now, she stood in front of Curtis' desk, arms rigid at her sides.

"Why do the sisters want to talk with me?"

"They run the *La Casa de la Gente*."

"Yes, yes, I'm aware of that," said Curtis interrupting Alicia, although he knew little about the *Casa* except that it existed to help the poor.

"Well, as you probably know, they outreach in the communities, give people in need a place to stay, emotional support, and provide clothes and household goods families need. They're Catholic sponsored, but they assist anyone—Christian, Buddhist, anyone in need—no matter their religion."

"Right, and…" said Curtis moving his hand in a circular, hurry-along gesture.

"They want to talk with you about the vigil, offer suggestions on how to bring our town together against violence," said Alicia, in a rush of words.

"All right, just give me a few minutes and then I'll see them."

Curtis wasn't Catholic, but there were times, when he was a boy, that he recalled seeing the nuns who taught at the school near his house. Those nuns were clearly recognizable with their black and white head coverings. They wore plain, dark shifts over long-sleeved blouses. Except for the crosses that hung on chains around their necks, the two nuns now residing in his lobby looked like any other conservatively-dressed women.

Sister Clarice, when Alicia introduced them, was a tiny, wizened woman with brown, wrinkled skin that looked like she had spent most of her life outdoors. She smiled when she shook Curtis' hand, and the wrinkles folded around lively brown eyes. Bright, perfectly-straight teeth made Curtis wonder if they were real. Sister Beatrice, on the other hand, was a tall angular woman with silver-streaked blonde hair that she wore combed back from her face. She offered a large boney hand for Curtis to shake, and he felt the strength in her grip. Sister Clarice spoke first.

"Alicia told us you were going to hold a vigil for Marcela Gomez, the young girl who was killed. We'd like to participate on behalf of the mission."

Curtis looked to where Alicia's desk sat in the corner of their office, but she had quietly slipped out the door after the initial introductions.

Tonight, looking at the large crowd gathered in the gymnasium, he suspected Alicia knew exactly what her talk with the priest would instigate. The audience sat in distinct groups. In the front were the city's governmental body along with the mayor and business owners he recognized. Behind them sat a group of mostly white citizens—farmers and their wives in worn blue jeans, and others still wearing workday attire. On one side of the gymnasium was a cluster of Hispanics. Some families had resided in the area for several generations. They came to work for the railroad or in the sugar beet fields and, over time, integrated into middle class neighborhoods. There were also the transients, some here illegally and some on work visas. They worked in the packing plants or at low paying jobs: washing dishes in restaurants, as maids, or in the fields as hired hands.

On the other side of the gymnasium were the Vietnamese and other Asian residents. They were the newest immigrants. They had come to America, sponsored by area churches, after South Vietnam fell. They were the ones fortunate enough to have the funds or connections to ease their way out of Vietnam. Later, the boat people arrived and were assigned to settlement camps. When the U.S. Government offered tax incentives to businesses that hired these refugees, they migrated west to work at beef packing plants in Kansas, Oklahoma, and Nebraska. They moved where jobs were available, rarely staying long enough to integrate into the communities.

Curtis looked at his watch again. Seven o'clock. Time to start the meeting. He rose to stand behind the podium.

"Hello, Hello." Curtis said. He tapped the microphone to make sure it was on. It whined. Both the crowd and the microphone settled into silence. Curtis wiped sweaty palms against his pants. He cleared his throat, the sound rippling through the air. A few people giggled at the rude noise.

Curtis began. "I want to welcome you all here. We have a bigger crowd than expected. Dr. Kline wasn't able to attend, so I'll make the introductions. But first, I want to acknowledge the tragedy that brings us here. Marcela was only seven years old when she was gunned down a little over week ago. It was a tragedy that has torn apart our town and highlighted the problem we have with drugs and gangs. I knew Marcela, in fact I talked with her shortly before she was killed." Curtis's throat tightened on the last sentence. He refused to look at Alicia, sitting in front with her husband and children, but he could imagine her sharp look, the truth in her eyes.

He continued with the short speech. He had closeted himself in Mark Kline's office seeking inspiration and quiet so he could compose what to needed to say. Unable to find the right words, he pulled open one of the drawers in Kline's desk. Inside was a folder labeled, "speech notes." Inside were notebook pages with handwritten quotes and stapled pages that looked like they were torn from a magazine. Curtis thumbed through the contents, pulling out a few phrases and quotes.

Kline must have been a fan of Thoreau and Dale Carnegie because many of the quotes were attributed to them. There was even the old Robert Frost poem, *The Road Not Taken*. Curtis remembered the Frost poem from high school. He thought about using it but decided it didn't fit with this occasion. He jotted down a couple of quotes. Dr. Kline had drafted a few paragraphs of a speech and Curtis copied them too, changing words here and there. Was it really stealing to use someone else's words if that person was the one who was supposed to lead the meeting? He hoped not. He'd acknowledge Dr. Kline and, of course, the authors of the quotes. He wasn't dumb enough to think he could cull those words and call them his own. The themes, though, he'd be okay tweaking those to use.

Curtis stopped speaking for a minute and looked out at the audience. Lord, it was hot in the gym. It felt even hotter standing behind the podium with all eyes on him. He took out a handkerchief and wiped his brow. He resumed speaking but then felt a shift in the air. It was as if someone was behind him, whispering, their cool breath on his neck. He paused for a moment, listening. Then the cool breath was inside him and Curtis claimed ownership of the words, the ideas, he had co-opted from Dr. Kline notes. When he told the audience, "We need to move past hurts we have inflicted on others and others have inflicted on us," he felt the heaviness of his words that had wounded Marcela's spirit. When he said, "The hurt will never disappear, but we can build something stronger out of the ruins," Curtis felt an airy tendril of redemption, even forgiveness, drift through the stuffy gymnasium.

Later, after everyone left and he had locked the doors, sat the alarms, and gone home, Curtis thought the discussion had gone well. After his short speech, he introduced the panel and just let them run with their ideas. All and all, it had gone well, except for a question from one man in the audience.

The vigil was scheduled for Wednesday evening, a week away. They'd start with candles and prayers by a priest at the church Marcela had attended. Then they would ask the Vietnamese Catholic priest and a Buddhist priest, and, possibly, the Methodist minister from the downtown church to say a few words. After the benediction, the vigil would take on a different tone, a positive tone to celebrate a new community spirit, all members coming together to stitch a new community fabric. This new community, the mayor had said in his speech, will come together to weed out the law breakers from the neighborhoods. Curtis wasn't sure about that. The cultural enclaves tended to shelter their own, especially from law enforcement. He wondered if anyone stepped up to identify the boys who shot Marcela. The old Vietnamese colonel said his people were appalled at the actions of their own. Maybe the members of those shuttered enclaves wouldn't talk to authorities, but Curtis bet they knew who was responsible for the girl's death.

8

Rochelle

Rochelle leaned against the cool, block wall of the hot gymnasium. The noisy, industrial-size fans pulled cooler air from the hallway into the gym, but it provided miserly relief. Twice, a man opened a double door leading to the outside, and to fresher air, but each time the community center's maintenance man came by and closed the door.

"I'm surprised at the number of people that came out," said Juanita, in a nasal tone. Juanita owned the sewing alterations shop next door to Rochelle. She was a pot-bellied woman with gray skin and hair. Her back was permanently hunched from working over a sewing machine nine hours each workday.

"Me too," said Rochelle. "Guess it always takes a tragedy to make people decide they must come together."

"Amen. Not that some vigil gonna make everything peachy. There's lots of bad stuff, bad people if ya really want to know, been coming to my city for a long time now. I was born here, you know, lived at the edge of town when I was a kid. Course now, the place where my folks' house was is surrounded by city. They's new, expensive houses with perfect green lawns, and where is everyone? Inside watching the damn T.V., that's where. Back when I was growing up, kids played outside all summer. Nobody worried about them getting into gangs and fighting like that. My mom had this old cow bell mounted on the front porch and when she clanged it, we knew it was time to come runnin'."

Rochelle wondered if time had eroded Juanita's memories, carving away the jousting to be in the popular group, or the merciless teasing and bullying that kids always did, and leaving only pleasant memories of warm summers with the days lazily rolling out in front of her.

"Guess things were different for you?" Juanita said, looking Rochelle over.

"Yeah," said Rochelle, leaving it at that. Juanita came into the shop occasionally. She looked at Rochelle's jewelry and asked about remedies for her crooked, arthritic fingers. Juanita had tried a couple of mixtures Rochelle made for her but said the pills her doctor prescribed worked better. Now, Juanita came in to buy saltwater taffy and to finger the necklaces Rochelle made. She'd wind the silver chains with their bright beads around her swollen fingers. Rochelle wondered if playing with the jewelry, with its shiny beads and fluid silver, reminded the old woman of her youth, when both her back and her fingers were supple and straight.

Rochelle scanned the audience searching for Jim. She found him standing against the back wall surveying the audience for any signs of trouble. He was in his uniform this evening, a visible presence meant to keep the peace in the crowd. He caught her eye and tipped his head in acknowledgement, but didn't smile.

She hadn't talked to him since their argument, two days ago. Not that they talked every day, but this silence was different. The connection she always felt with him, like a thick chain, seemed to have cracked a link; the bond no longer reliable. She watched Jim greet people as they walked by. She watched him for any mark their argument had left. Was there a melancholy in his face between greetings? Did she only imagine there was a forced gaiety in his smile? He was far enough away that she couldn't pick up the nuances of his interactions, but whenever she looked over her shoulder at him, he quickly focused on her. Perhaps their connection was intact after all.

Curtis walked to the podium and tapped the microphone. Rochelle turned her attention to the stage.

At first, his speech was jerky. Sweat beaded Curtis' head making it glisten under the lights. Twice, he blinked rapidly behind his glasses and, only then, did he pause for a moment, remove his glasses and wipe his face and head with a paper towel. First, Curtis introduced the members of the panel to his left and right, stumbling only a little on Truong Van Duc's name. Rochelle knew Colonel Duc. He'd often been in her shop looking for a remedy for the blood rash on his hands, common in plant workers who, for hours, handled bloody cow parts. Most of the time her customers were hesitant, first looking at the T-shirts and wares and, finally, working their way toward the drawers at other side of the store, where the aromatic roots and dried plants were kept. But when the old Colonel came in, he went directly to the drawers. He bent over the counter and carefully read the labels that identified the the contents. He told Rochelle, in slow precise English, what he needed. There was no discussion of his symptoms, with Rochelle leading the conversation toward what the customer needed for their ailment. Duc knew what he needed; only the difference between the Vietnamese name and the Latin or common name Rochelle knew it by hindered the quest.

Duc had been a colonel in the South Vietnamese Army, he told Rochelle. He was an ambitious soldier, well into his rise through the military ranks, when the American military evacuated him, his wife, and their three children and brought them to America. He was too valuable, the military told him, to leave him to the cleanup forces of the North Vietnamese conquerors. Duc had fruitful hopes, when he landed in the country of opportunity, to join the American army. But his efforts had fallen short of his expectations. The war was winding down and, despite assurances from the American personnel who had worked with him in Vietnam. There was cynicism about the patriotism of a man who looked so much like the enemy.

Duc was trapped in the same net that encompassed all his people in this new country of opportunity—teachers, engineers, rice farmers, fishermen—both the educated and the uneducated. They all struggled to learn a new language and find work. He told Rochelle that he was one of the lucky ones. A Lutheran church in Western Nebraska had adopted his family and guided him toward employment that, although beneath his abilities, provided a steady income. His children quickly learned the language and assimilated into American culture. One of his daughters was now a professor at a California university and his son was in college studying to become an engineer. Only the eldest daughter had stayed close. Colonel Duc still worked. He worked to fill the lonely space left after his wife died. He worked so he could maintain his independence and demonstrate to his children and grandchildren that America was still the land of opportunity, if one was willing to make the effort.

Rochelle turned her attention to the front of the gym. Curtis finished introducing the panel and began talking to the audience. At first, he read from his notes, addressing the podium, instead of the audience. Some of the phrases and quotes Curtis used were ones she had heard Mark Kline use.

"Life is not a smooth road, but if one aims high, the difficulty faced will hone the traveler, steady their steps, and make it possible to reach the summit." It was a phrase Dr. Kline favored when he wanted to move the community to action.

There was the Thoreau quote that was Kline's favorite, "You cannot dream yourself into a character; you must hammer and forge yourself into one."

Rochelle studied the audience, gauging their reaction. Some sat attentive, others whispered to the person sitting next to them. Parents shushed restless children. She studied Curtis. She saw him pause, his head cocked as if listening to something only he could hear. He lifted his face, and it seemed to Rochelle that he connected with his audience for the first time. There were still Dr. Kline's words and phrases that scattered through Curtis' speech, but it was as if he had assimilated the sentiments behind the familiar quotes, rather than just parroting someone else's words.

The audience seemed to notice the difference. All eyes were now on the speaker. Rochelle glanced at Jim. He, too, was focused on Curtis. A faint smile tugged the corner of his mouth. He must have felt Rochelle's eyes on him, because he turned to look at her. Jim twitched his eyebrows at her, the smile still tugging a corner of his mouth.

Other members of the panel took their turn. The nuns, Rochelle had seen them before but didn't know their names, talked about their service in other countries. They recounted how they assisted Guatemalan citizens who lived, precariously, between the country's military and the guerillas trying to overthrow the ruling class. They talked about working in India, amidst the impoverished and isolated lower caste citizens. Then Colonel Duc talked about his experiences and the needs of the Vietnamese community. Although Rochelle knew his colonel status held no sway in America, the close-knit Vietnamese community still recognized his rank as well as the similarity of their struggles in this new land. The speakers spoke of the same theme—people displaced, both inside their new community, and from their home lands.

At eight-thirty, the meeting broke. The audience had become restless in the hot, crowded gymnasium. Parents with sleepy, cranky children were the first to leave when Curtis rose to wrap up the meeting. Those who stayed raised their hands with questions for the panel members.

Rochelle watched the crowd. She saw heads nod in agreement, both when the questions were asked of the speakers, and when they were answered. She saw a young man in tight jeans, his forehead pale where the cowboy hat, now held in his hand, normally perched, shake hands with a young Hispanic man herding his family toward the door. A Vietnamese woman placed her hand on the arm of a stooped, white-hair woman, and they bent their heads together in conversation. Watching them made Rochelle hopeful. She, too, turned to go. Her feet in the thin-soled sandals were hot and sore from standing so long.

Rochelle heard music as she exited the gym, following a group of parents with cranky children. She couldn't make out the words of the Latin music but felt the base beat from the car stereo pulse in the air. Parents pulled their children close and picked up the youngest ones to speed their way to the parking lot. Rochelle looked south, toward the source of the music.

A block away, a group of teenagers stood in the street beside older model, American-made cars. The cars had been modified so they sat low to the ground. They glistened where light from the streetlamps struck polished paint and chromed wheels. A group of boys leaned against the cars, smoking. When they brought the cigarettes to their lips to pull the smoke, Rochelle saw their thin faces in the reflected red glow of the cigarette tips. Girls with long dark hair; high, black-paint eyebrows; and short jean skirts stood in front of, or leaned against, the boys. One girl arched her back, hips pressed tight against the boy's groin. She giggled and lightly smacked him on the arm. Their voices rose and faded under the sound of the music, their words indistinct.

Rochelle watched them as she crossed the street. She saw one of the girls point at the people exiting the community and say something to her companions. They laughed. In the middle of the street, Rochelle slowed, flipping her hair over her shoulder, to show them she wasn't afraid of their posturing. She stepped onto the curb, then heard other music, metallic sounds with a staccato beat. The sound of electric guitars overrode the Latin beat. Two cars, compact and fast, Toyotas or Datsuns, sped from the cross street between Rochelle and the Latino group. The cars slowed when they entered the intersection. Immediately, the group from the parked cars alerted. Four young men stepped in front of the girls, feet apart, chests thrust forward. Some flashed gang signs. Others stuck up their middle finger. One of the boys went to the car's open window and reached inside. The girls, all flirtation vanquished, shifted to the sidewalk, putting vehicles between them and the newcomers.

The two foreign cars sped through the intersection. Then, Rochelle heard the screech of tires. The cars reversed, backing through the intersection and stopped. Quickly, Rochelle turned the key in the shop's door lock and stepped inside. Ducking low, she scrambled in the dark to the cordless phone behind the cash register. Crouched behind the counter, she started to punch in 9-1-1. But, before she could complete the sequence of numbers, she saw Jim come outside. He was watching the activity in the street and talking on his mic. People had started to pour out from the community center door. They looked down the street at the cars and the shouting groups and froze. Jim stepped away from the crowd and motioned to the people already outside to move further down. People on the way out the door reversed and went back inside.

The two groups continued to shout at each other. One shouted from their position in the middle of Abilene Street. The boys in the cars stopped in the intersection leaned out the windows. Then, someone yelled, "Cops." Heads popped back into the Toyotas and Datsuns. Tires screeching, they vanished down the side street. For a minute, everyone stood frozen. Then, the Latino youths began talking and moving animatedly. The crowd in front of the community center scurried to the safety of their vehicles and home.

Rochelle checked the lock on the shop door again, only then becoming aware how fast her heart beat and the sweat forming in the small of her back. She slipped behind the wall that separated the shop from the stairs leading to her apartment. Upstairs, she watched through the window as the last of the crowd left. Only when the last stragglers left the lot did the group of Hispanic youth climb into their cars and leave, their audience gone.

Rochelle kicked off her sandals and laid down on the bed waiting, hoping, that Jim would call. She fell asleep, the rotary fan sweeping air in the quiet room.

Curtis

◇

Once again, visitors were waiting for Curtis when he arrived at work. Sisters Beatrice and Clarice sat in the lobby, heads together, talking quietly. He glanced at the clock on the lobby wall. It showed two minutes before eight. At least this time he wasn't late to work. Sister Clarice had a spiral notebook open in her lap. As he walked by, she jotted something in it. Curtis strolled quickly past them, his eyes forward like he hadn't seen them, and rounded the reception desk where Alicia sat. Out of sight of the nuns, he pointed at them and mouthed to Alicia, "Why are they here?" Just like the first time, Alicia rose and followed Curtis into the office.

"They want to talk with you, again," Alicia said, in a whisper.

"Why me? You told me you'd coordinate the plans for the vigil."

"Yes, I told them that, but they said they want to talk with you about something else."

"What about? Anyway, I'm not even Catholic."

"I know that," said Alicia, frowning. "Just talk with them."

"All right, then, all right."

Curtis drummed his pen on the desk blotter waiting for Alicia to usher the nuns in. He hoped whatever they wanted to tell him wouldn't take too long. Dr. Kline had called him at home last night. He asked Curtis to come to their house for a lunch but hadn't provided an explanation for why he wanted to see him.

"It's hard for me to get out of the house," Dr. Kline had said. "Come by at noon and we'll have lunch together. My wife makes an excellent chicken and tomato salad."

Curtis had agreed; hadn't really had an option, or a ready excuse, for why he couldn't come. He had hoped for time to prepare, time to try and anticipate the conversational direction, but first he had to deal with these pesky nuns.

Had someone made a complaint to the old man about the center, or their vigil plans? Worse, did Kline want to question Curtis about the girl's death? Was the old director thinking about retiring? It was about time. He hadn't been to work since Curtis took over and that had been months. If so, was Kline going to recommend Curtis for the job to the center's board or was he just going to tell him about his replacement? Curtis wished he knew Kline's intent. If he knew, at least he could prepare. But first, the early bird nuns.

Sister Clarice began the conversation after the sisters were settled on the hard metal chairs in Curtis' cramped office. "We were happy to see such as great turnout at the community meeting. We believe the event will be a positive one for our city." She smiled at Curtis, the browned skin around her eyes forming thin wrinkles. Curtis wondered how old she was. Her restless energy and military straight posture belied the sun-damaged face and grey hair.

"Your community center is such an asset," she continued. "Alicia gave us a tour the other day. Lots of activities, and the open-court basketball on Friday evenings is a great way for both parents and teens to play ball together, get involved."

"Yes," Sister Beatrice said, continuing the conversation without pause, "and your daycare is a great help for working parents. I noticed they have an educational component as well as recreational activities."

"It's a good way to enhance learning during the summer months, keep the children's minds and bodies sharp and ready for school in the fall," said Sister Clarice, deftly receiving the conversational baton from the other nun. Curtis wondered, first, where the conversation was headed and, second, just how practiced they were at this tag team approach.

"Thank you," said Curtis.

"Yes, we like the daycare. I understand you have a couple of openings there?"

"Well, I guess," Curtis said. He didn't know much about their day-to-day operation. "You'd have to talk to Susie Nguyen, she oversees the daycare."

"We did when we visited," said Sister Beatrice, taking up the baton again.

Again, Curtis wondered where the conversation was headed, but before he could figure it out, they switched topics.

"Do you know much about our organization?" asked Sister Clarice.

"Ah, no."

"Sister Beatrice and I members of the Missionary Sisters of Christian Charity Order. We are assigned to various communities in different countries; anywhere there is a need to assist indigent immigrants assimilating into new places or cultures."

"Sister Clarice and I have been worked, either together or alongside other members of our Order, in Guatemala, Canada, and India."

"Canada?" Curtis started to ask.

"Wherever we're needed," finished Sister Clarice.

"We've been here in Kingston for almost two years," said Beatrice.

"We oversee *La Casa de la Gente*," said Clarice. "It translates, the home of the people. We're in the old hotel on the corner of North Main and Atchison streets. Are you familiar with it?"

"I seem to recall…." began Curtis. He shifted in his chair. He tried to avoid that part of the city. It had once been the vital center of old Kingston City. The abandoned brick hotel sat near the railroad tracks that used to carry supplies and visitors. Now, the area consisted of several abandoned warehouses with boarded up windows. There was a liquor store and a rundown shop that sold well-used furniture and other household items. People with dirty hair and old clothes shambled down the streets.

They made Curtis uncomfortable, so he normally stayed away from that area of town. Last time he was through, was it a year or more ago, he noticed trucks and vans parked in the street around the old hotel. Signs on their doors identified the vehicles as belonging to construction companies, heating and air conditioning firms, and plumbing contractors.

"*La Casa*, offers a food pantry and social services—housing, medical, and dental assistance—to those in need," said Sister Clarice.

"I'm assuming by the name you mostly cater to…" he began, but the nun interrupted.

"We provide assistance to anyone who comes through our doors. No matter what country or religion."

"In fact," said Sister Beatrice, beaming a smile, "we have a couple of single mothers and their children staying with us. The old hotel rooms on the second and third floor have been made into temporary housing for the unhoused. The second floor is where the mothers and children stay. Of course, they're separated, you understand, from the men we house on the third floor."

"Sure," said Curtis, into the pause in their conversation.

Beatrice and Clarice exchanged a look.

"The reason we want to speak to you," began Clarice, "s that we have two children we'd like to place in the daycare. Their mother is starting a new job, and..."

This time, Curtis happily snatched the opportunity to interrupt their conversational flow.   "You'd have to talk to Susie Nguyen about it," said Curtis. He should have been preparing for his meeting with Kline and here he was, forced to handle something he had no responsibility for. He started to rise so he could usher these two out and onto to Susie, who they should have talked to anyway, but before he could stand, Sister Beatrice said.

"The mother has just started her job. She doesn't have the funds to pay for daycare. Her two children are five and six. Being homeless, their education has been sketchy the last year. The schooling your daycare provides, as well as the interaction with other children their age, would be beneficial for them."

"Like I said, Susie manages the daycare," Curtis said again, and this time Sister Clarice was the one who spoke.

"A couple of daycare scholarships, perhaps? It would help immensely."

"I'd have to bring it up at the board meeting, I can't just..."

"Of course, we understand. I think I saw a list of your board members somewhere. Do you recall where, Sister Beatrice?"

"Yes, I think I saw their names in a newspaper article we have back at *La Casa*."

"Oh sure, I remember now. Seems like there were a couple of names we recognized from Saint Augustine Church and from Saint Guadalupe."

"You're right, Sister Clarice. We can give them a call about the scholarships."

They both looked at Curtis and smiled, Clarice's twinkling brown eyes disappeared into the dry folds around her eyes. Beatrice's eyes, blue as a Kansas summer sky, gleamed below thick blond brows.

Curtis looked from one to the other, measuring how it would play to the center's board. If he rejected their request outright and they went behind his back to convince the board members to offer a scholarship, it would look bad for him. On the other hand, if these nuns imposed their will on the church supporters, they might antagonize the board members enough to support Curtis' decision to deny the scholarships. On the other hand, if Mark Kline was considering retirement, maybe proposing a daycare scholarship to the board would demonstrate to them that Curtis would be an innovative director. He was still mulling over the possibilities, and the pitfalls, when Sister Beatrice spoke.

"Mr. Myerson, why don't you come by *La Casa* and see what we do. Maybe, that would help in your decision."

"That and, perhaps, a little prayer for inspiration," said Sister Clarice.

"I guess I could," said Curtis. It would buy him some time; see how his visit with Mark Kline went. He'd stall for a few days and, if he was lucky, wouldn't have to go.

"Great," said Sister Beatrice. "See you tomorrow then?"

"Well," said Curtis, but that was all he had a chance to say.

"It was nice seeing you again," said Sister Clarice popping up from the chair and extending her hand to shake so nimbly that Curtis wondered once again about her age. "We'll look for you tomorrow morning."

Curtis thought about the nuns' visit as he drove to Mark and Emily Kline's home. He felt, not for the first time since he started working at the Community Center, the subtle pressures that nudged him, cajoled him, to grudgingly go beyond his comfortable position as interim manager—marking time until a better job offer came along. There was the complicity he felt in the girl's death. True, she was a pest bothering them every afternoon, but he had taken pleasure in her discomfort. Curtis didn't often attend church, hadn't gone to Sunday services since he and Amy separated.

After he died, he'd have to appear before heaven's gatekeeper and account for his life. Would he be able to counter the bad things he had done in his life with good intentions? Was intent enough or was it only action that marked a tally on the heavenly side of Saint Peter's tablet? The nuns, even his daughter Melody, seemed to believe he was a better man than he felt inside.

The previous Saturday, he and Melody were browsing the bookstore—Melody wanted yet another book about horses—and they ran into one of the center's daycare boys and his mother. Curtis couldn't recall the boy's name, but his red curly hair and the pale freckles that marched across his nose and checks made him memorable.

"Hi, Mr. Myerson," the boy said when he caught sight of Curtis. His mother nudged him, and the boy stuck out his hand and said in a formal manner, "I'm Kevin and it's nice to see you again, Mr. Myerson." Kevin's mother beamed, and Curtis guessed they had practiced the greeting. He introduced Melody and they all chatted for a minute about the center's activities and upcoming vigil.

Melody didn't say anything about the exchange until they were in the car on their way to the ice cream store. She glanced at her dad a couple of times as he drove, a puzzled look on her face. It made Curtis wonder, not for the first time, what his ex-wife was saying about him.

"Was that one of your daycare kids?" asked Melody.

"Yes, for the summer. He goes back to school in the fall."

"He doesn't look poor. I thought just poor kids went there."

Curtis turned from his driving to look at Melody. "We have all kinds of kids come to the center," he had said, "all colors and economic levels."

"Oh," said Melody, the puzzled look still on her face.

"Daddy?" she said, a few minutes later. "Did Kevin know the girl that was killed?"

"Probably."

Melody was quiet. Curtis glanced at her and saw the pucker lines between her brows that in his daughter always signified deep thought.

She said, "I want to go to the vigil with you. Can I?"

10

Rochelle

———◈———

Rochelle sat in the lobby of the police department waiting to be called. She watched as, one-by-one, people walked to the reception window and spoke through a round hole in the Plexiglas. Some murmured in low voices; others spoke in loud, anxious tones. Occasionally, the uniformed officer behind the window buzzed opened the door, but mostly, he motioned them to take a seat in the lobby. Rochelle watched and pretended to read a magazine. A smell of desperation hung in the air. There was a man with oily hair and dirty hands who rocked back and forth in the chair. Newcomers sat as far away as they could from him, his stench and conduct erecting a barrier between him and the rest of those waiting. A young woman that Rochelle estimated was barely out of her teens, with long hair and a bruise from eyebrow to cheekbone, was trying unsuccessfully to make two toddlers sit still.

"Mikey, sit. Now," she hissed, pulling on Mikey's arm to try and get him back onto the chair.

"You, too, Annie. Damn it. Calm down." She put out her arm to block Annie from climbing down from the other chair after her brother.

"Mommie, pee pee," said the girl.

Rochelle stood, put the magazine back on the table and went to sit down beside the boy the young woman had called Mikey.

"Twins, I'm guessing," said Rochelle.

"Yeah, and they're driving me up the wall. Now, with everything else," she waved her hand at the glassed reception booth, "I'm trying to potty train them."

"I can watch this one while you take her," said Rochelle.

The woman looked at Rochelle with narrowed eyes. Rochelle didn't know if she was assessing her ability to manage the squirming toddler, or if she was determining whether she could trust a stranger to watch one of her children.

"Okay, just be a minute," the woman said. She lifted the girl onto her hip and hurried toward the restroom door.

The toddler looked at his mother disappearing into the restroom, and then at Rochelle. He stuck out his lower lip and his face crunched up. Rochelle picked up her handbag and ruffled through it, trying to find something to ward off Mikey's looming wail. Immediately, the boy's face relaxed as he watched, curious. Rochelle pulled out a pocket notebook and pen she always carried and opened the book to a blank page.

"Do you like puppies?" Rochelle asked.

The boy nodded.

Rochelle held the notebook between them so they could both view it. She drew a line figure of a dog. Mikey leaned against Rochelle and watched. She could smell the clean scent of his soft hair. Rochelle added a high tail and perky ears to the dog.

Mikey pointed to the dog and said, "Spots."

Rochelle added patches and filled them in with black ink. Mikey looked at her and smiled. He turned his attention back to the notebook, one of his hands toying with the bracelet that dangled from Rochelle's wrist.

Rochelle was shading in the dog's eyes when the mother reappeared; Annie again perched on a hip.

"Rochelle Sanchez," a uniformed woman announced when the door opened beside the reception window.

Rochelle stood and finger waved a goodbye to Mikey and his mother.

"Come with me," the officer said.

She led Rochelle through a maze of cubicles and offices. Rochelle heard the ring of phones and the mummer of voices. One cubicle she peered into contained a man dressed in a short-sleeved white shirt and tie. He was banging away on an old typewriter. She looked for Jim, but didn't see him.

The officer walked down a short hall with closed doors on each side. She opened one of the doors and motioned Rochelle in.

"They'll be here in just a minute," she said and then left, closing the door behind her.

The room felt claustrophobic. There was a small desk pushed into one corner of the room with two chairs on the long side of the table, and one chair on the short side. The walls were painted pale gray and the linoleum floor looked as worn as the table and chairs. Rochelle studied the setup, guessing a suspect would be assigned to the single chair at the short end of the table. She selected one of the other chairs, the one closest to the door and sat. She tucked her legs under the chair and then reconsidered. She placed them in front, crossing one leg over her knee in a gesture she hoped looked confident.

The door opened and Jim walked in, followed by another man, this one in a shirt and tie.

"Ms. Sanchez, good to see you again," Jim said. He stepped forward to shake her hand. He held her hand for a moment longer than expected and his eyes, to Rochelle, seemed warm and friendly behind the formal greeting.

"Thanks for coming in," said the other man, shaking her hand for a shorter, more customary time. "I'm Detective Patterson, and I understand you've already met Officer Nicholas." He looked at Jim, but Jim still had eyes on Rochelle. Detective Patterson shifted his gaze between Jim and Rochelle and frowned. He motioned for them to take a seat. Rochelle retained the seat by the door. Jim sat down beside her and Patterson sat in, what Rochelle had predicted, was normally the suspect's chair. She gave the detective what she hoped was her most disarming smile and turned to Jim. She hadn't seen him since their argument. Now, he sat beside her, and she could feel the warmth of his body and smell the musky scent of the aftershave he always wore. For the first time since she had been summoned to the station, she relaxed.

"Your description to Sergeant Nicholas of the suspects in Marcela's shooting was helpful," said Patterson, taking control of the interview. I understand you also witnessed an incident between two groups of youths the night of the meeting at the community center."

"Yes," said Rochelle.

"We have some questions for you. Perhaps you can help fill in details about both incidents. I also have some photos to show you. See if you recognize any of them as being present when Marcela and Antonio Gomez were shot."

Rochelle told them what she remembered. Twice. Each time, the detective and Jim asked questions that teased out a fuller picture for them. The headshots they showed Rochelle didn't display the cocky attitude and swagger she had seen the Vietnamese teens exhibit the afternoon Marcela was shot, but she recognized the hard eyes, angled cheekbones, and narrow face of the shooter. "That one and that one were there, but I didn't see who actually fired the shot," she said, pointing out two photos in the ten they showed her. She wasn't sure about the other. There had been another boy, she told them, but those two, Rochelle pointed at the two photographs she recognized, "These are the ones I remember seeing, both walking through the neighborhood earlier, and at the time of the shooting."

The morning visit to the police station exhausted her and afternoon business in the shop was slow. Rochelle tried to string glass beads to make a necklace, but she was restless and couldn't concentrate. She kept glancing up at the clock, but time crept like a turtle toward six o'clock.

Finally, it was time to close and make her way up the stairs to the privacy of her own apartment. She poured a flute of Zinfandel and sat in the chair by the back window. Recounting the details of the afternoon when the shooting happened to Jim and the detective had made the memories of that afternoon come alive again. A tear dripped down her cheek. She took the napkin that she had wrapped around the wine glass to hold in the chill and wiped her eyes.

It had felt good to sit beside the little boy, Mikey, and listen as he told her the puppy she drew needed spots and short, upright ears. She remembered the sweet child scent of his hair as he leaned against her.

Marcela's mother had been right, Rochelle could never birth a child, but if she had the last surgery, obtained a new birth certificate that showed her gender as female, and no trace of the boy child remained on her, could she persuade an agency to let her adopt some abandoned and unwanted child? It wouldn't have to be a baby. After all, what did she know of infants, but surely there were children out there who longed for a mother the way she had begun to long for a child.

That wasn't the only reason she felt morose. She was stuck in a rut. Sure, the shop served a purpose. Her minimal living expenses were covered by the profit she made, and she was proud of her success, but some of the joy she felt flipping the sign in the window from closed to open had dissipated. And there was Jim. He loved her, that she was sure of, but would he still feel the same after her final step to womanhood? Witnessing Marcella's death made her realize how unpredictable life was.

The phone rang. Rochelle startled at the sound. She rubbed the last trace of tears off her face with the damp napkin and picked up the receiver.

"Hello," she said.

"Hey, baby. It was good to see you today," Jim said, in a low soft voice. "I miss you. Okay if I come over for a while?"

11

Curtis

———◇———

Mark and Emily Kline's home was warm and stuffy. The thermometer at the bank had flashed 99 degrees when Curtis passed it on the way to their home, and the air was unusually humid. He entered the Kline house anticipating the cool dry air of air conditioning, but they must still use a swamp cooler. The coolers were great for dry, desert heat, but ineffective in the steamy atmosphere of this day.

Their house reminded Curtis of visits to his grandparents when he was a boy. A grandfather clock sat in the entrance, the movement of its pendulum a visible reminder of time passing. The close air smelled of years of fried meals overlaid with a faint musty smell that he always associated with homes where the elderly lived.

Emily Kline answered the door. "My husband will be here shortly," she said.

When Mark entered the room to greet Curtis, he was shocked at how the man looked. True, Dr. Kline was in his early seventies, but he had been a vigorous seventy in the photographs Curtis had seen. Now the man looked old and frail. He leaned heavily on an aluminum cane when he walked. The skin was tight over cheekbones and his eyes were hollowed and dark. Mrs. Kline was the opposite. Although she, too, was in her seventies, her walk was quick and light. Her hair was coiffed into a blond helmet, and she wore a warm coral lipstick.

The chicken salad, as Kline promised, was delicious, with a tangy dressing served on fresh sliced tomatoes and topped with slivers of toasted almonds. Emily Kline, wrapped in a sweater, even in this warm house, beamed when Curtis complimented her. Conversation centered on the community center and what was happening day-to-day.

"We were very disheartened to hear about little Marcela's death," said Mark. "I remember her. She was a little mite when she first came to the daycare, just starting to toddle." He turned and smiled at his wife. "All those administrative duties tried me and when I became bored with it, I'd walk around the center. Visiting the daycare was my favorite part of the day. We are fortunate that we have a great staff there. They are so enthused about the children. And the children are delightful, so honest and open."

Mrs. Kline smiled at her husband. Mark took a bite of his tomato and chewed, thoughtfully.

"Emily and I have lived in Kingston for thirty years, and I've been with the center for twenty of that. We lived in New York City before. We both taught in the Queens' borough schools—both elementary and secondary schools. Now that was a lesson in how different peoples can live and work together. And what a rich cultural mix we enjoyed: Indian and Greek restaurants, all the different art galleries and museums, jazz and blues music and, of course, New York Mets baseball.

"We miss that great ethnic mix, those windows into other cultures." He paused, smiled at his wife. "But, after we started our family, we thought it best we come back to the middle of the country to raise the children. Emily's parents were in Wichita then and mine were in Denver. We wanted a smaller town," Mark smiled at Emily, "closer to the grandparents. Right, honey?"

Emile nodded. "Right in the middle, between both sets; close enough to visit but not close enough for in-law interference."

Curtis participated in the conversation but wondered where it was going and why he had been summoned. Kline said that it was important that he come, but did the old man just want an audience so he could reminisce about the places where he had lived and his work at the community center? It felt like he was wasting time. Was this what he would do in his old age—fish around for someone to listen to him talk about how it used it be? And what would he say? He had lived in this town all his life, worked at a job where it felt like he was just marking time. Marking time waiting for what? During pauses in the conversation, Curtis could hear the tick of the grandfather clock in the next room, its chime marking out time in quarter hours.

Finally, they were done with the meal. Curtis was thinking up ways to politely leave this stuffy house when Mark Kline spoke.

"Curtis and I are going to sit outside for a while and talk. Could you please bring a couple of glasses of iced tea out to the patio for us, dear."

Curtis was surprised when he followed the shuffling Mark out of the house to the patio. A tall Chinese Elm tree arched over a shady bricked area. A cool breeze rustled the leaves. A wrought iron table and two chairs sat in one corner where the shade was deepest. There was a pile of folders on the table held down with an angular quartz rock.

Mark held onto both cane and table as he lowered himself into a chair. The effort to walk outside and sit down seemed to have exhausted him, and his face looked even waxier in the natural light. He took a drink of the tea that Emily carried outside and Curtis noticed a tremor in his hand as he sat the glass down. Then, as if gathering strength from somewhere inside his failing body, he looked at Curtis and smiled. When he spoke, his voice was clear and strong.

"A friend of ours was kind enough to record the speech you gave at the center. I thought you did a good job. In fact, a couple of things you said were similar to what I would have said if it were me—things meant to bring people together, and motivate them. I especially liked it when you said vital goals are accomplished by people who keep trying, even when there seems to be little hope."

Curtis looked away and tried not to blush. Except for a word or two he changed, he'd pulled the phrase from one of Dr. Kline's old speeches. He wondered if the old man knew he had appropriated his words, or if the character of the sentence simply struck a chord of recognition.

He looked at Kline. Dr. Mark Kline, still the wily old goat, was grinning at Curtis. He waited to see what Curtis had to say. Curtis took a deep breath before he spoke.

"I went through some of the speeches you had in your files. I didn't know, really, what to say. I apologize."

Kline waved a hand, interrupting Curtis' apology. "Don't fret about it, young man. I co-opted those words from Dale Carnegie. I always liked Mr. Carnegie, used a lot of his quotes myself. In fact," Mark leaned his head back and closed his eyes, drew from his memory, "Dale Carnegie himself said the ideas I stand for are not mine. He would say, I borrowed them from Socrates. I swiped them from Chesterfield. I stole them from Jesus. And I put them in a book. If you don't like their guidelines, whose would you use?"

Mark opened his eyes and smiled at Curtis. "I've decided to retire. It's about time. The doctors aren't optimistic about my ability to return as director." Mark looked down at the thin legs splayed out in front of him. When he looked up, the smile was gone, and his eyes were once again hollow and dark in their sockets.

"It's hell when one's will is as strong as ever but the body, well, the body is sick and worn out. I haven't submitted my resignation to the board yet, but I plan to this week. Listening to you talk at the meeting, if you're interested, I'd like to recommend you to the board to replace me."

Curtis' heart leapt. He hadn't known why he was summoned to the doc's house. He had worried about being fired. Maybe, the old director had heard about the way he treated Marcela on the day she was shot. Then he worried that the old man was angry that he co-opted his words. But here was this unexpected offer, like a gift. His throat tightened. He couldn't think of what to say.

"I'm interested," Curtis finally managed to choke out. He hoped he didn't sound too eager.

"Of course, it will be the board's decision," Kline said. "I can't speak for them, but I will make the recommendation if you're interested."

On the drive back to work, Curtis envisioned himself in Kline's old office, settled in the deep leather cushions of the desk chair. It would be Curtis' name on the name plaque outside the door. It was about time his luck changed.

12

Rochelle

R ochelle was sweeping the floor with her back to the door, so she didn't see who came in.

"Be there in a minute," she said, when the bell above the door announced she had a customer. She brushed the debris into the back corner. It was out of sight, and she'd sweep it into a dustpan later, after this customer left. Rochelle leaned the broom against the corner and turned to greet the customer.

She jumped and put her hand to her chest when she saw who had quietly slipped through the store until he stood behind her.

"Shit, Antonio. You startled me."

Antonio's face was tight, and she could see paleness under the tan skin. It looked like Antonio had lost twenty pounds and gained ten years since Rochelle last saw him, the day Marcela was killed. He leaned heavily against the counter, holding the side where he had been shot.

"Sorry," he mumbled.

"What are you doing here, anyway? Weren't you just released from the hospital? What has it been now, eight or nine days?"

"Nine," he said.

"Here, take a seat. Looks like you need it." Rochelle pulled a tall chair from behind the counter. Antonio struggled to pull himself onto the high seat. Rochelle stepped close to help. His long dark hair was pulled into a band at the back of his neck. Sweat, either from the outside heat or exertion, beaded at his hair line. Rochelle grasped Antonio's elbow, and she felt the sinewy muscles in his arm. He had a clean scent, like cotton with a faint medicinal undertone. Rochelle breathed the scent in, enjoying his warm fragrance. When Antonio was finally seated, she pulled up another chair and sat in it, facing him. The young man was handsome, she saw up close. Long dark lashes framed eyes the color of sun-dried raisins.

Get a grip, she scolded herself.

She waited for Antonio to begin, unsure why he was here.

"My mom came to see you." Antonio began.

"Yes," said Rochelle, not knowing if it had been a statement or a question.

"She said she appreciated your concern, what you said about my sister, about her not suffering." Antonio's voice trailed off and he gazed out the window at the door of the community center, "After what happened."

Rochelle didn't think Lucia's attitude had been appreciative that day, but she wasn't going to unlatch that Pandora's Box.

"Lucia, your mother, she's doing better?"

Antonio shrugged. "Better, maybe, but my mother will never be well. The family, my sister and brother, are gone too. Marcela was her last hope."

"She still has you," said Rochelle.

Antonio barked a laugh, the sound harsh in the quiet store. "Yeah, she still has me." He put a hand to his side, as though the laugh had pained him.

Rochelle sat quietly. Normally, she would steer the conversation like her uncle did, nudging the customer toward the kernel of need that had brought him into the shop. But Antonio made her uncomfortable, and her physical reaction to him, the intimacy of their meeting in the early morning hours before the busy activity of customers could provide a distraction, did not permit her the objectivity she needed.

Antonio shifted to look out at the street. Then he turned back to face her, his head cocked to one side. "You saw what happened in the street, then."

Again, Rochelle couldn't tell if it was a question or a statement of fact. He was there, he knew what happened. She did not want to be a part of any scheme he was concocting.

"Some of it," she answered. "I was busy with a customer and didn't see everything. Then the shooting started, and we ducked. Everything happened fast. I was more worried about the customer getting hurt. It was a scary moment."

Rochelle shut up, realized she was rambling. Her heart pounded and Antonio's closeness made her squirm. She wanted to scoot down from the chair and move, diffuse the intensity between them. She felt not at all like her normal self.

"Did you see who shot my sister?" Antonio asked, looking straight at her, pinning Rochelle's eyes with his.

This time, there was no mistaking that it was a question, or the purpose of Antonio's visit.

Rochelle held his eyes, gathering strength for the telling. What she planned to say wasn't a lie, but it wasn't the complete truth either.

"Like I said. And like I told your mom. I was helping a customer, not watching what was happening outside, until the shots were fired. Then we hit the floor. I don't know exactly who shot who."

Rochelle straightened in the chair, mentally forced her mind away from Antonio's bad-boy charm—the touch of his arm under her hand, his clean, male scent.

"And my window was shot too. That means someone from your side of the street fired back. Who do you think was shooting back, Antonio? You or Marcela? And what was the argument over, do you think? Who sells their dope on this corner or that?"

Antonio glared, a fierce look on his face now. *This is his warrior's face*, Rochelle realized. It was the face of the organizer who was rumored to run shipments of cocaine and marijuana from Mexico and coldly sell them to the lonely and disenfranchised living here, far from their family and homeland.

Antonio slid off the chair, wincing when he landed. He limped over to the wall of drawers and pulled one open. Pulling out a cloth bag, he opened it and poured granules of a dried green substance on the glass top of the counter. Rochelle wanted to tell him to stop. She wanted to tell him that she was the only one who handled the contents of the drawers. But there was rigidness to Antonio's posture and his expression when he looked at her that stilled her tongue.

"What's this?" he asked.

"It's ground Evening Primrose plant."

"What does it do?"

"It helps relieve a woman's PMS symptoms."

Antonio hissed. He swept the granules off the counter, dismissing both the remedy and the feminine complaint. He glared at Rochelle and opened another drawer. He pulled out a dried brown nub. A thick mass of thread-like roots made it look hairy and alien.

"What about this? What does it do?"

"It's dried Valerian root. It alleviates stress and pain. Helps with depression and anxiety."

"All this," Antonio said, waving his hand at the bank of oak drawers, "makes people feel better? Like an aspirin or something a doctor orders? Well, so does weed."

Rochelle caught the weed comparison, and it angered her that he was comparing addictive illegal substances he sold to remedies designed to heal and soothe.

"These," she waved a hand at the drawers, "have medicinal components. Remedies used long before the invention of modern drugs."

"Right, but now they have better drugs, but still, you sell this." He opened another drawer, scooped out tiny black seeds and poured them over the glass countertop. The round seeds bounced on the glass and spilled across the floor.

He smirked. "Seeds and weeds."

Rochelle trembled. She was frightened, but damn if she let Antonio see her fear. He rounded counter and moved toward her. Rochelle refused to back away.

"There's a psychological component too," said Rochelle, "a belief in their powers that reaches back to a different time. That's just as important.

"Uh huh, right." said Antonio.

"And, these," Rochelle pointed to the seeds still rolling off the counter to the floor, "don't make someone rob a convenience store so they can buy more."

Antonio stopped in front of her. He was the same height as Rochelle and so close she could see the tiny hairs sprinkled across his nose. Gold striations radiated from his pupils, through the darker brown of his irises.

Antonio cupped his hands around Rochelle's shoulders and then ran them down her arms to her elbows, and back up again, over her shoulders to her neck, and further up to cup her face. Rochelle froze. Her heart pounded and she felt a tightening, like liquid fire, in her groin. Damn him. She tried to stop her knees to stop knocking.

Antonio said softly, "I loved my sister. If I could, I would trade places with her. It'd give my mom a cry, but she'd know she kept the best one."

Rochelle felt a tear well, then slip from her eye. She didn't know if it was tension or his closeness that suddenly recalled the bright memory of Marcela, lying still and bloody in her brother's arms.

Antonio took his hands away from Rochelle's face. He brought a finger to his lips and licked the tear that had run down Rochelle's cheek and onto his hand. Rochelle shivered. Antonio noticed. He grinned, but the eyes remained hard. Then he turned and walked away. When he pulled the door open the bell above the door gave an excited jangle, loud in the quiet shop.

Rochelle stood for a few minutes, afraid her legs would betray her and she'd fall if she tried to walk. After a moment, she went to the refrigerator at the back of the shop and pulled out a can of Coke. She popped the top and took a long swallow. Her hand still shook, but she wasn't sure if it was from fear of Antonio or fear of the excitement she felt when he held her face in his hands.

13

Curtis

Curtis sat on an old church pew in the lobby of the *Casa de la Gente* mission, waiting to be summoned. The pew was made of wood, darkened by age. Deep scratches on the thick legs told of much use and rough travel. The bench seat was smooth, though, polished by years of churchgoers slipping from the pew to kneel or rise.

The building that housed the *Casa* also had a history. It was the old Walden Hotel, a six-story brick hotel that rose high above the flat plains. In early years, it was a welcoming beacon for stagecoach and train passengers traveling west from Kansas City to Denver or California. The elegance of the once grand building still showed in its high, pressed-tin ceilings and wide, wood trim, inlaid with carved rosettes at the corners of windows and doors. Now the building smelled musty. The odor of people lost and friendless hung in the air.

Curtis wondered how long the nuns would make him wait. Was it payback for him making them wait when they visited his center or were they just busy. He watched as people shuffled in, exhausted by their slide toward poverty and homelessness, and were ushered down a hall. Were the sisters, altruistic by profession and calling, also skilled in games of one-up-man-ship or politics? He wasn't Catholic, but he knew the church could not have grown into the powerful entity it was without some willful manipulation of parishioners and governing bodies.

He hadn't wanted to come, tried to put off the nun's invitation to visit the mission, but his visit with Mark Kline had changed his focus. He wanted the center's directorship. It was a good stepping-stone back into business management. He'd work there a few years, make contacts in the community, and then shift away from community work back into the real workplace.

He enjoyed the perks a management position in a private company offered: a car he didn't have to worry about maintaining, travel to places where he stayed in upscale motels, talking with similarly-ambitious people, and golfing on Saturday mornings. Best of all, he could move out of the stuffy closet they called his office and into Kline's with the window and soft leather chair that rolled smoothly up to a large desk.

There was the beautiful shop owner across the street. She'd brushed him off when he went over to visit, but if he became director, she would see him in a different light. He'd be the successful man who managed a youth center and a daycare, a community leader who talked with groups and visited places like the mission. She'd loop her arm through his and gaze at him with admiration. Her dark hair and eyes and warm complexion would be good for his image too. It would demonstrate that he was accepting of all people, unbiased. They'd hold hands across the table in a fine restaurant and kiss on a moonlight walk. It had been a long time since he had someone to care about, and to care about him. It was lonely watching television every night in his tiny apartment where six steps carried him from kitchenette to the doorway of his bedroom.

"Mr. Myerson?" someone said, dragging Curtis back into the *Casa's* lobby.

"Yes, I'm Curtis Myerson," he said to the young girl. She was dressed in a plain cotton skirt and white blouse buttoned to her throat. She was not at all like the sultry woman of his daydream.

"Good, come with me."

She led him down the hall, their footsteps echoing in the high space, and into a large office. Cluttered desks sat facing each other on opposite sides of the room. File cabinets stood in orderly rows. A round table with three chairs perched between the desks. Sister Clarice sat behind one of the desks. She rose as Curtis entered.

"We're glad you came, Curtis," she said, taking his hand in both of hers.

"That's all, Maria," Sister Clarice said to the young woman who had ushered Curtis in. "You can go, just leave the door open, please."

"Yes, Sister," Maria said, with a quick bow.

"Maria is one of our convent novitiates working with us this summer. She's been a great help," Sister Clarice explained after the girl left. "Come, let's sit at the table. I don't like speaking to someone from behind a desk." She waved at her desk, cluttered with papers and books.

"Sister Beatrice was going to join us, but we had a situation come up with one of our resident families and she's busy," Sister Clarice said, after they settled in chairs at the round table. Let me tell you a little about our mission and then we'll take a tour. May I assume that you've reached the decision about offering a daycare scholarship to a couple of our children?" She smiled at Curtis, the skin around her eyes crinkling until only the dark pupils were visible.

"I mentioned it to Dr. Kline. He's in favor of it but, of course, it must be vetted and approved by the Center's board. We won't be able to do that until the next meeting." Curtis held up his hands in an *it's out of my control.* "The board will have to formally approve it. I'm sure you understand how that works."

"I see," Sister Clarice said, slowly. "And have you had a chance to discuss it with the daycare manager, Ms. Nguyen?" This time her eyes were steely. Curtis remembered, too late, that the sisters had already talked to Susie. He had mentioned the scholarship to Kline but forgot to say anything to Susie. The nun's eyes bored into him, like she could see all the other things he'd left undone or relegated to the bottom of the list.

Curtis tore himself from what he suspected was a stare honed by years of imposing hers, and the church's, will. An open Bible lay on the edge of Sister Clarice's desk. Was it there for show, or did she refer to it? He turned back to the nun and steeled himself.

"As I said, the scholarship has to first be approved by the center's board of directors. I'm sure Ms. Nguyen will be on board with the idea, but it has to be formalized."

"We understand," the nun said. She fingered the gold cross that hung on a chain around her neck. "We'll expect to hear from you soon, Mr. Myerson. Come, let me show you around our *Casa de la Gente*."

Driving back to work, Curtis composed how to explain it to Susie. They had an uneasy alliance fueled, he was sure, by Alicia's gossip about his performance. He'd present the idea of the two scholarships, taking a firm approach like the director he was going to be. First, he'd outline the reasons why this would be a positive move for both the community center and the Catholic mission. Next, he would gently insist, persuade, deflect any argument she had. If there was still resistance, he'd invoke the name of Dr. Kline, tell her that this was something Kline supported. He'd make it work.

Curtis passed a Burger King. He was noon and his stomach rumbled when the smell of meat sizzling on a grill reached him. He pulled into the Burger King drive and queued up in the carry-out lane behind the other customers. He saw a girl about his daughter's age walk out with her mother and felt his heart squeeze. The girl reminded Curtis of Melody and their visit last Saturday.

"Dad," Melody had asked, "when is that vigil thing you're having?"

They were sitting on a park bench eating ice cream cones. Curtis had ordered two scoops, one chocolate and one pistachio, his favorites, and he was eating fast before the ice cream melted and ran down the cone and onto his hand.

"Next Wednesday," he said. "Wednesday evening."

"Can I go too?" Melody asked.

He had looked at his daughter, her hairline damp with sweat from the heat and her orange and blue mouth, stained by the tropical fruit sherbet in her cone. He loved his daughter, had loved her since the minute she arrived, red and squawking, into his life. Sure, he'd had a few setbacks— loss of his job, the problem at the bar, a marriage he couldn't resurrect, but Melody was perfect, even with her awkward walk and a voice like her mother's.

"It's okay with me, but we'd better check with your mom."

He had checked with Amy, and it had not gone well, at least initially.

"I don't think it's a good idea with all that's gone on around the Center," said Amy. She stood in the entryway of their home, arms crossed, barring entrance. This was the house where they had lived before the divorce. Now, he was a stranger there. He had to ring the doorbell and beg permission before being admitted to this both familiar and alien space.

"It'll be safe. There's going to be lots of police to keep an eye on things, make sure everyone's safe. I heard Sheriff Folsom is even going to be there."

"You mean fat, old Gerald Folsom who hasn't drawn a gun since he was elected to office twenty years ago? Lot of damn protection that will be." She laughed, maybe at the vision of Sheriff Folsom waddling after a suspect, gun held in one chubby hand.

Curtis cleared a suddenly tight throat. "Melody wants to go and I think it'll be good for her. You're the one who said she was upset when she learned about the shooting from the news. It'd be good to have her witness how the community comes back together, heals."

"That's a crappy part of town and you know it. Lots of illegals come over the border, cause problems, and then just flee back to Mexico. They just want to tangle it up with the boat people that came from 'Nam. You think that you," she waved her hand above her head, "or anyone else can protect my daughter from that?"

"Amy, is everything okay?" came a voice from the back of the house.

Amy looked back over her shoulder and Curtis saw a man in baggy khaki shorts and no shirt walk out of the kitchen. He held a glass in one hand, a sandwich in the other.

"Oh, hey there, Curtis. Ah, good to see you again."

"Mike," Curtis growled. He couldn't believe it—his old golfing buddy, Mike McPherson, looking way too comfortable in Curtis' home. His former home, anyway.

"We're fine, just talking. I'll be there in a minute," Amy said, turning back to face Curtis. Her face was flushed. She had better be embarrassed at being caught with his old friend.

"That's cozy," said Curtis, motioning toward the living room where Mike had gone.

"He's just a friend," said Amy.

"Right," said Curtis, drawing out the word.

"We're divorced now, remember. I can have my own friends."

"Ah hum." He was afraid if opened his mouth he'd say something that he would later regret. Sure, they were divorced, but Mike? This was his golfing buddy with whom he'd shared beers and complaints about their jobs and women. Mike, who laughed when he farted loudly, and told coarse stories about the women he dated. He closed his eyes for a minute, blocking out the image of Amy and Mike in the same bed he once shared with his wife.

"Well, I guess if there's going to be law enforcement and lots of people around, it might be okay," Amy said.

She had never liked the silent moments that sometimes fell into their conversations. She always had to fill the empty air with prattle, reluctant to allow contemplation. This time, it worked to his advantage.

"Yes," Curtis quickly agreed. "Melody and I'll be okay." He rushed on, using Amy's discomfort about Mike to his advantage. "I'll pick her up about four. Then, I'll have her back to you by ten o'clock at the latest." He shut up, realizing he was the one prattling now.

Waiting in the drive-through line to place his order at Burger King, Curtis wondered why he hadn't mentioned Mark Kline was going to recommend he be appointed director. Curtis wanted to give Amy a dig, let her know he still had potential. He wasn't a loser, as she had shouted at him at the end of their marriage. Maybe, he didn't tell her because her awkwardness about being caught with the half-dressed Mike was dig enough for one day, a tally on his side of the post-divorce ledger.

Curtis examined his face in the rear-view mirror. The car's air conditioner, running at full force in its battle against the hot interior, tossed around the thin strands of hair on top of his head. He'd lost thirty pounds since the divorce. In the bathroom mirror at his apartment his stomach looked leaner and the heavy jowls had receded. Now, in the car mirror, he saw the deflated jowls hung loose and his eyes appeared bruised from lack of sleep and stress.

The car ahead of him pulled forward. Curtis pulled up to the order box and rolled down the window.

14

Rochelle

Rochelle sprayed Windex on the glass-topped display case. She set the spray bottle on the floor and picked up an old dishtowel, softened with use. Using a circular motion, she wiped fingerprints and dust off the glass. Then she moved to the front of the cabinet and did the same thing. The store seemed brighter this morning. The new store front window the glass company installed yesterday afternoon let in the light, unlike the sheet of plywood put up after the bullet round shattered the old window. After she cleaned the glass cases, she used the damp cloth to sweep the dust from the deep window ledge that ran along the front of the store. She gazed outside as she dusted.

There was scant evidence left of what had happened at the Center. The candles, photos, and stuffed animals of Marcela's memorial were long gone, collected, she supposed, by family or friends. The wilted bouquets of flowers had been either tossed in the trash or their loose petals pushed into the street by the dry wind. There was nothing, except for a scrap of paper in the gutter, to give witness to that horrible afternoon. Rochelle wondered which was better. Was it better to keep photos, candles, and flowers that grimly testified what happened, or was it better to scrub away the ugly reminders, leaving only happy memories of the girl.

Rochelle took the Windex and dishrags back to the storage closet. Returning, she enjoyed the way the light sparkled on the clean glass cases. How bright the light looked through the new window. The three remaining windows looked dirty next to the new one. She looked at the clock on the side wall. It was a little after eight. Most weekday mornings, customers didn't start arriving until nine o'clock or so. There was plenty of time to wash the dirty windows. She went upstairs to her apartment and filled the bucket she kept under her sink with hot water, then added vinegar and a dribble of dish soap. She carried the bucket outside and went back in for towels, a long-handled squeegee and a ladder from the storage room at the back of the store.

The first pane was almost finished when Rochelle felt a change in the air. The sky had dawned bright and clear as Rochelle sat at her dinette table reading yesterday's newspaper and drinking coffee. As she cleaned, a few puffy clouds flitted across the sky and cast shadows in the street. Now, the normally dry air felt heavy and wet. Looking to the northwest, Rochelle saw the horizon had turned a deep blue, like a storm was brewing over Colorado and Nebraska.

She was finishing the second pane when the air shifted again, a breeze coming from the east. The humid breeze brought the smell from the beef processing plant ten miles east of town. It was a scent putrid and familiar, organic with a mixture of manure and decay, intermingled with the pungent odor of the cooked blood and hides that were turned into pet food. Everything in a cow: flesh, bone, blood, hair was used in some way. The stink made Rochelle's stomach clinch.

Except for her time in Miami, this ugly odor surrounded her. It reminded her of her childhood. *Abuela* Angelina made her uncles and older cousins shower and leave their work clothes and boots in the shed out back of their house. The clothes were cleaned in the ancient washer and drier in the shed, not allowed to contaminate the family laundry inside the home. No matter what precautions were taken, the smell of raw meat, blood, and curing hides still seeped into their home. It floated out of opened lunch boxes and from between the pages of the paperback novels read on breaks. The smell seeped into the skin and nostrils of the men, day after work day, until no amount of soap and scrubbing could vanquish it.

Rochelle rarely ate beef, and never pork. She wondered if the families who grilled hamburgers in their backyards, or businessmen in suits forking up fat marbled streaks steaks ever gave thought to how the red chubs of ground beef or slabs of red meat arrived at markets and restaurants.

Rochelle moved the ladder in front of the third and final pane. She lifted the pail to the top of the ladder and, tucking the squeegee under one arm, climbed the ladder's rungs. If *Abuela* Angelina hadn't called Rochelle, pleading with her to come home and help after she received a diagnosis of the cancer that would kill her six months later, Rochelle would have stayed in Miami. Here she was, ten years later, still breathing in the processor plant's foul smell, still hiding her secret, wedged between her childhood as a boy and the future as a complete woman.

Why didn't she leave? Angelina was gone as was Rochelle's own mother. Her mom had taken off, with her latest boyfriend to where she didn't know, long before Angelina got the cancer.

Rochelle knew of a cousin and his family living in Tulsa, but they had never been close. She didn't know where her brother, Lewis, lived. He was older, had children, likely grandbabies by now. They hadn't been close as children. Lewis wanted to play softball in the street and Rochelle preferred reading or playing by herself. The only time she visited from Miami, Lewis had looked her over with her tight pants and patterned blouse with a scooped neckline.

"*Punta*," he had called her spitting in the dirt beside her shoes. "You leave a boy and what do you return, a disgrace on your family."

"Pay him no mind, *Mija*," said her *abuela*. "He's his father's son, no manners and few brains." Rochelle hadn't seen Lewis again until Angelina's funeral. He huddled in a pew with his wife and her family on the other side of the church sanctuary and left as soon as mass ended.

Every few months, Rochelle brought flowers to Angelina's grave. She'd scrub off the bird droppings from the granite headstone and brush dried grass clippings from the base. Then she'd replace the faded silk flowers in the vase with new ones: red Poinsettia rosettes in the winter, pink and yellow tulips for spring, and big yellow sunflowers with brown middles in the summer. If her *abuela* had other visitors, they left no sign.

Was that the only thing that kept Rochelle here in the middle of this flat farm country? No, there was the shop. She had sold Angelina's house and property, used the money to purchase the building and merchandise. The shop had done well for her too. She'd never make enough money from the remedies, jewelry, and other items to survive in a large city, but she made enough to pay the overhead and property taxes, and tuck a few dollars away each month in her savings account.

Jim also tied her to this town. She had met him at the hospital when Rochelle was there to visit Angelina and he had come to interview a car wreck victim. He was her friend, her lover, the one person to whom she could reveal her dreams. If only. That was what Rochelle always circled back to. If only, they could catch a movie without Jim fretting about what people thought. If only, he wasn't so committed to his work and his sister and her children. What Rochelle loved about Jim were the same things that kept them apart.

It wasn't just Angelina's illness that brought Rochelle back. There was also the memory of Eduardo that had caused her to flee Miami for the calm safety of Angelina's home. Eduardo with his burning eyes and thin, tense body. His family had emigrated from Cuba, before Castro slammed shut the border between his island country and the free world. Eduardo was born in America. His father, a wealthy businessman in Cuba, came to America and expanded his wealth by means one should not examine too closely. Rochelle met Eduardo at one of the candy-colored, neon-lighted gay bars on Miami's beach. The wiry and agile Eduardo was like a tiger that thrilled by prowling through a jungle village, knowing any minute one of the villagers could step out from behind a tree or a hut and fly an arrow into his heart. They zoomed around Miami on his Ducati racing motorcycle, Eduardo folded over the tank and Rochelle pressed tight against his back. The breasts she bought were new then, and she thrilled with the feel of them against Eduardo's hot back. The strum of the motorcycle's engine sang through her core.

Eduardo leaned low into winding highway corners, pitting centrifugal force against gravity. It was on one of those nights, when Eduardo, alone in the early morning hours, lost the battle with gravity and wreaked. Rochelle saw the news report of his accident on the evening news. After the news crews and investigators left, she drove to the site where he died. The asphalt road was slippery where the wind had blown sand from the beach onto the pavement. A gouge in the asphalt ran off the road and deep furrows in the sandy soil told of Eduardo's flight and tumble. Rochelle picked up an amber signal light, bruised and scratched from the crash. She still had it in the back of her closet. It was a reminder of how fickle were both fate and gravity.

She stepped back from the window, checking to see if she had missed a spot. It had become overcast. Gray sky reflected silver in the clean glass. She looked up, suspecting it was going to rain and spot her clean windows. Folding the ladder she carried everything back inside.

It was mid-morning before she had her first customer. Others soon came, made their selections, paid, and left. It was late morning when two girls entered, the bell giving a welcoming ring when they opened the door.

"How much are these?" one girl asked, holding up a pair of pink flip flops with a yellow plastic flower on the strap.

"Oh, those are so cute," said her friend drawing out the "o" in so. "Is there a blue pair?"

"I think so. They're normally nine dollars," Rochelle told her, "but this week they're ten percent off."

Rochelle guessed the girls were sixteen or seventeen. School began in a couple of weeks and these two girls were one of several clusters that had come looking for sunglasses, summer shoes, and T-shirts inked with beach scenes. They bought summer items as if their purchases could postpone the coming school year with its books and constricted schedules. Rochelle was glad to see the shoppers deplete her summer inventory. It meant less merchandise to discount as summer faded to fall, and sandals and T-shirts were no longer desired.

"I'll take these," the girl said, putting the pink sandals on the counter. "And these too," she said, laying a pair of sunglasses and two candy bars beside the shoes." She looked at Rochelle from beneath long lashes.

"Eighteen dollars and sixty-three cents," said Rochelle. "That includes the ten percent discount on the shoes." She took the twenty the girl offered and counted back the change.

The second teen placed her selection on the counter: a pair of blue and white striped flip flops and a cotton shirt with sea turtle scene printed on the front.

"I love your earrings," the second girl said.

"Thank you," said Rochelle. She pointed to the display case of jewelry. "I make jewelry. There's a better selection over there, if you want to look."

"Oh," said the girls in unison. They went over to look at the display.

Rochelle watched them as they leaned on the glass display case to look, elbows resting on the top. She smelled their coconut-scented tanning lotion and figured she'd have to wipe greasy prints off the glass after they left. The first girl had long, straight, light-brown hair clasped in a pony tail at the crown of her head. The second girl had short, curly red hair that she kept trying to smooth with her hand.

"I bet the silver hoops with the turquoise beads would look great on you," Rochelle told the red-headed girl.

They asked to look at other pieces and Rochelle brought the jewelry out, piece by piece. They held the earrings against their ears and turned their heads this way and that as they studied their reflections in the mirror. The brown-haired girl, Becky, the red-headed one called her, kept gazing behind Rochelle, at the wall of drawers.

"I heard you have all kinds of cool stuff in the drawers," Becky finally said, pointing to the drawers.

"Yes, I have herbs and other natural ingredients that I used in remedies."

Both girls giggled. "Herbs?"

Rochelle grinned and shook a finger at them. "Not that kind of herb. Did you know that the component in today's aspirin first came from willow bark? People knew way back in Hippocrates day that it was helpful in reducing fever and relieving pain."

Rochelle went to a drawer and pulled out a leathery brown root. "This is goldenseal root. I grind it into powder and mix it with one of the oils for skin infections and insect bites. It's also used internally to help with mucus problems."

She pulled open another drawer, took out a cloth bag and shook out a few dried particles. "This is dried comfrey leaf. I make a tea with the leaves and sell it as an antiseptic gargle for sour throats. That's what I have, old natural remedies for pain, stomach upset, skin diseases. That type of herb." She looked at the girls and smiled.

"Do you have something to make a guy fall in love with me?" asked the red-haired girl.

"Like a love potion, you mean?"

"Yeah, like that." The girl said.

"Well, honey, if I could mix up something like that, I'd sell the formula for a million bucks and be lying on some tropical island beach." Rochelle paused for a minute. "You never know, though, the mind is powerful. I can fix something up that would make you believe you're falling in love, but it's something you'd make happen, not something that affects the actions of others. Easier to change yourself than someone else, you know."

The girl with the red hair, Amy was her name Rochelle learned, selected the silver earrings with the turquoise beads Rochelle recommended. Becky selected a necklace made of delicate gold links and glass and copper beads that went well with her honey-colored hair and skin. They paid for their purchases and left, but before Becky stepped through the door, she looked over her shoulder at the drawers of mysterious substances. Rochelle knew from the look that her curiosity had been sparked. She would be back.

It was after one thirty in the afternoon before Rochelle had a chance to dash up the stairs to her apartment and make a chicken salad sandwich.

She was washing her hands at the sink in the back of the store when she heard the bell over the door sound. She turned around and saw Colonel Duc walk in. She assessed him as she walked toward him. He had always been lean and wiry, but today he looked gaunt. His face, below protruding cheekbones, was shrunken and his eyes were rimmed with dark circles. The old colonel's posture had always been straight and proud, but today his shoulders slumped, and his walk was not the sure stride she remembered.

"Colonel Duc," she said in acknowledgement.

"Ms. Rochelle," Duc said, giving a little bow.

"Are your hands bothering you again?" she asked. He had come to her before with the complaint. She doubted that was the problem today, but she needed a starting point.

"No, not today. Today is a bigger problem. My grandson, Truong, was arrested last night. The police, they say he was one of the boys who shot the girl there," he motioned across the street at the community center door. "They come to my daughter's house, took my grandson away, and searched the house. In his closet they find a gun."

"Oh, no," said Rochelle. "Come, have a seat. Tell me what happened." She went over in her mind the faces of the boys who had stood on the sidewalk in front of her window, yelling at Antonio and flashing gang signs with quick movements of their arms and hands. One of the boys, she recalled now, had the same sharp cheekbones as the old colonel, but none of his proud bearing. Was he the shooter? She'd been crawling across the floor to pull Valerie down and didn't see who fired.

"I came because the police officer I talked to at the station after Troung was arrested said you witnessed what happened."

Rochelle froze. She had lifted her hand ready to pat Duc on the shoulder, offer comfort. Now her hand stilled.

"Yes, I saw some of what happened." She wanted to say more but wasn't sure where the colonel was going with his question. Would he ask her to tell the police that now she wasn't sure what she had seen? Duc lived through years of war in his country. He had to be ruthless, as well as brave, to have climbed to the rank of colonel. Was this old man still ruthless enough to force her into a lie?

It was too late for that. She had already told the detectives what she saw. Plus, Jim, with his steely eyes, always saw through to the truth and would recognize the lie in her memory lapse. No, she would say nothing more, force this old man to ask his questions. She held herself still, searched his thin face.

Duc straightened his spine. "In my country, I fought many years to keep my family from harm. The war was difficult, fighting an enemy that looked like yourself. An enemy who ate the same food, observed the same holidays, grieved loss in the same way. Then, I come to America where anything is possible, but here the enemy is subtle. This enemy battles from the inside—inside ourselves, our families, our customs. This enemy I don't know how to fight."

Rochelle nodded.

"In America, there are great possibilities, if one is willing to work hard. But it is also dangerous to our way of life. In this country, a person is independent; they do not learn to sacrifice so that the family can prosper. The enemy arises from within the family, its core, rather than from outside."

"Yes," Rochelle agreed. She thought about her own family, each member going their own way; the core of her family, Angelina, unable to hold the family true.

Duc turned from Rochelle, gazed out the window, as if divining his future in the busy street. After a minute, he pulled his eyes back to her. She remained quiet, hands in her lap, still not sure where the old colonel was leading her. He may not be sure himself.

Duc patted Rochelle's hand and rose. "I came in for more of your salve for the rash, but I realize now I won't need it."

Rochelle's heart beat faster. Was this proud man going to end his suffering, his life, because of a grandson he felt responsible for?

"Colonel, what do you mean you won't need it?" she asked.

Duc searched her face for a moment, and then light dawned in his eyes. "No, no," he said quickly. "I'm going to give up my job at the plant. I'll be seventy-two years old this month. Perhaps, I have a little time remaining to help my grandson." He looked away and then back at Rochelle, his eyes determined. "You have always been an honest person. Do what you must do."

It was his last words that told Rochelle what she suspected, his real motive for seeing her. But he hadn't asked what she had seen or hinted that she shade the truth to make Truong's actions less damaging. She didn't know why he changed course but was glad he did.

Rochelle watched Colonel Duc leave, the bell above the door making a forlorn sound in the quiet shop.

15

Curtis

———⬦———

Curtis, here's a draft of the agenda for tomorrow afternoon. I need you to look it over, see if there's anything you want to add."

Curtis was surprised Alicia was talking to him. She was already working at her desk in their shared office when he arrived this morning. Her back had been to him, and she ignored his greeting when he came in. Periodically, she would leave, and he would hear the printer hum outside the office door.

"Agenda?" he asked, unsure what his assistant was talking about.

She made the quiet huffing sound, air expelled through her nose, like she always did when something aggravated her. Curtis doubted Alicia was aware of it. Their office space was so cramped he sometimes heard the sound when she was on the telephone or, more often, when she spoke to him.

"The agenda for the meeting to finalize plans for the vigil," Alicia said. "I've already notified the attendees, but you have to name the issues." She glared at him, huffed through her nose again. "You do remember the vigil that we're holding next week." She spoke the last sentence deliberately and slowly as if he was a dim-witted child.

"Yes, of course," snapped Curtis, attempting to reclaim the boss status. "We have a couple of meetings on tap this week. I just wasn't sure which one you were referring to. Just put the agenda in my inbox and I'll get to it."

Alicia didn't move.

"Yes?" asked Curtis, drawing the word out. This woman irritated him.

"The meeting is Friday. It's now," she looked at her watch, "Eleven fifteen, Wednesday morning. I need to have the agenda done early this afternoon so I can distribute it to everyone that'll be there."

"Alright, alright, hand it over. Who's supposed to be at the meeting anyway?" he asked.

"It'll be you, Susie Nguyen, me, and maybe Dr. Kline, if he's well enough to attend. There's the sisters, Beatrice and Clarice, from the *Casa de la Gente*, Father Frank from St. Guadalupe, and Father Trán, the Vietnamese priest who attended the community meeting last week. There are a couple of business owners from the neighborhood who offered to help. Michael Sorensen, he's the Kroger's Grocery manager, said they'll donate food and drinks. Let's see." She read the agenda, pulled her lower lip. "Of course, Police Chief McKinley and Sheriff Folsom will be there."

"What about that old Vietnamese captain or colonel, or whatever, who was on the panel at the public meeting. I can't recall his name." Curtis patted his shirt pocket, as if it still contained the slip of paper with the old man's name on it.

Alicia looked at him with the expression she always used when Curtis said something stupid.

"Colonel Duc?" she asked

"Yeah, something like that."

"Don't you watch the news? His grandson was one of the boys arrested for Marcela's murder."

"What?"

Alicia repeated it.

"Of course, I saw the news," Curtis said. He hated that his words sounded whiny, like a child who's been chastised for something he neglected to do. "So that was the colonel's grandson." The last was more to himself than to Alicia.

"Yes, I had him on the attendee list, but then I took him off."

"He asked to be taken off?" asked Curtis.

"No, but…" she started to say.

"Keep him on. If he doesn't come, fine. In fact, that will be even better. It puts the burden on him if he doesn't."

Alicia glared at Curtis. Fine, she should have asked him, instead of just assuming she needed to take the old man's name off. Curtis put out his hand to take the paper, but Alicia slapped it into his inbox, turned, and left.

"For God's sake," Curtis said under his breath. He could hear the clack of Alicia's shoes as she walked done the hall. To where, he didn't know, didn't care.

He hadn't missed the fact that Alicia still addressed him by his first name. She never called Mark Kline by his first name. To her, he was always Dr. Kline, his last name preceded by the title, doctor.

If Curtis was named director, the first thing he'd do is replace Alicia with someone who wouldn't look at him as if he was something distasteful they'd stepped in. He tapped a pencil on the desk blotter, envisioning the look on Alicia's face when he pink-slipped her. Then he stopped in mid-tap, thinking it through. He'd need Alicia to train the new secretary. He'd tell her, gently, so she'd think he was being generous. He'd claim he wanted to keep her on for a few weeks to help train the new girl. The pencil tapping started again. By then, Curtis would be in Kline's old office, settled behind the big desk. The new secretary would have her own space, apart from his, and Alicia, well, Curtis would relegate Alicia to the receptionist desk to train her replacement.

Curtis twisted the mechanical pencil through his fingers. He looked at what he had been reading before Alicia interrupted. The meeting was scheduled for Friday. Thursday was the community center board meeting. He had been working on his resume. Had Kline had been in touch with the other board members yet, passed on his recommendation that Curtis be appointed the new director?

The evening before, Curtis sat on the minuscule patio outside his apartment and composed a list of his qualifications. He had more than twelve years of management experience at his former job. True, it was lower-level management, overseeing the manufacturer's line workers, instead of upper-management, where decisions were made that set the company's course. Still, management was management, and hadn't Curtis supervised the operation of the center the last few months?

He had dug through cardboard boxes crammed into the hall closet looking for his college transcript. The boxes contained his personal papers, those accumulated during the marriage and ones Amy didn't take in the divorce. There were photo albums of his family, and he spent far too long looking at the evidence of their old life. The young couple in the wedding photo looked happy, their faces toward the photographer, and beyond, to all the good years they knew lay ahead. In the old images he saw not himself, but a young, naïve man who believed a wonderful, successful life awaited him. There were also photographs of fat smiling baby Melody. Others showed her as a toddler, holding Curtis' hand and taking the first tentative steps into her own future. He closed the album when he came to the last image, he and Amy standing tense and far apart. They had quit snapping photographs about that time, afraid the images would reveal the conflict they tried to hide, even from themselves.

Curtis found a second photo album buried deep in the box. The plastic sleeve protecting the cloth and cardboard album was cracked and yellowed with age. Gingerly, he opened it, hearing soft crackles when he pulled the old cellophane pages apart. It was an album his mom must have pieced together before she became ill. There was a photograph of his mom and dad, both gone now, standing proudly in front of a black 1958 Chevrolet Impala. His mom wore a printed, white and pink summer dress with a narrow belt around her slim waist.

The photo gave Curtis a shock of both familiarity and strangeness. In it, his dad was grinning, and his arm was wrapped tenderly around his mother's waist. It seemed familiar because each morning in the mirror, reflected back, was his dad's high forehead and wide face with almost delicate lips. Curtis didn't realized he looked so much like his dad. The image felt strange, too, because what Curtis remembered as a child was not his father's smile and affection, with his arm proudly around his mother, but sternness and distance.

It was far from the easy affection his mother showed him and his brother, Simon. Curtis knew his dad cared about them. He demonstrated it by going to work every day before dawn, mowing the lawn to perfection in the summer, and on weekends when Curtis and Simon were out on dates, dozing in the chair in front of the television until they arrived home. But he had never hugged Curtis or his brother, or kissed them on their foreheads before sending them off to bed. After Melody was born, Curtis vowed he would hug his daughter often and kiss her every night before he tucked her into bed. He had done just that too. Now, despite his vow, he was relegated to weekend parenting: reading Melody a bedtime story, eating supper with her on his tiny apartment patio, and hugging her with enough affection to starve off his loneliness until the next weekend. He missed his family, missed being with Amy and Melody in his old house: Amy moving around the kitchen fixing dinner and Melody playing outside or sitting at the table doing homework.

Curtis put the photo albums back into the box and sat for a long time on the floor of the dusty closet, elbows on his knees and head in hands. Tears leaked through his fingers, and he angrily wiped at them. He was not going to cry. Crying meant accepting defeat and he refused to accept defeat.

He finally found the file with his college transcript near the bottom of the stack of boxes. The file now lay on his desk. He'd wait until Alicia went for lunch and then he'd make a copy of the transcript and diploma for his presentation to the board. He wasn't the best student, the transcript showed mostly Bs and Cs, but he had graduated with a degree in business and a minor in math. The education supplemented his work history. True, he had never worked around children before. Dr. Kline's doctorate was in some branch of education, but didn't being a father count in his favor? There was also the summer he was in high school and helped at the YMCA's children summer camp. He made another note on the yellow pad, "Experience teaching and supervising kids at summer camps." He scratched out "kids" and wrote in "students." It was only one summer and one camp, but the plural "camps" sounded better. Besides, he had helped with art classes, hiking adventures, and swimming lessons. Technically, he could classify those as separate camps. Besides, using the plural wasn't really a lie; it simply implied Curtis worked more than the single summer.

He heard Alicia's voice in the hallway outside the office. She was sitting at the receptionist's desk again, her refuge from their airless office. Either she was on the telephone, or someone had walked in the door. Curtis heard shuffling noises, like Alicia rising from her chair. Quickly, he put his resume in the desk drawer and pulled the meeting agenda from the inbox. Most of the invitees he knew—the nuns, priests, and ministers from the various faiths, and the Kroger manager, Michael Sorensen. He hadn't personally met the heads of law enforcement agencies, but he recognized who they were.

Curtis saw the name, Rochelle Sanchez. That must be the Rochelle who owned the shop across the street. Seeing her again would be good. He'd let her enter the meeting room first and wait until she selected a chair. Then he would take his place beside her making it look coincidental. He would even feign surprise to find himself settled next to her. He'd smile and say he was happy to see her involved in planning the event. Curtis remembered her scent, lemony with a hint of something sweet, Jasmine, perhaps. Rochelle would observe Curtis lead the meeting and realize how committed he was to the community. Later, he'd ask her to dinner so they could talk more. No, not dinner, that was too intimate. He'd ask her to lunch. They could eat sandwiches in the park down the street where the vigil would conclude with a picnic. An invitation to dinner would come after the vigil, after they learned more about each other.

Curtis heard footsteps outside the door and Alicia peered in.

"Have you had a chance to read the agenda yet?" she asked.

"Just finished," said Curtis. He hadn't read the whole thing but, despite the fact he didn't care much for Alicia's attitude, he had to admit that she did a thorough job with these kinds of things. He knew the grammar and syntax would be right, each word falling into its proper slot in the sentence. The spelling would be correct too. He handed the paper to Alicia.

"Looks good to me," he said. "Go ahead, make the copies and pass them out. Is everything ready in the meeting room? I thought refreshments might be good. Soda and lemonade. Cookies too."

Alicia took the paper and looked at it. A frown line furrowed the skin between her brows. "Nothing you wanted to change or add?" she asked.

Curtis realized she had noticed the lack of correction marks and scribbled changes.

"No," he said, forcing a wide smile. "Looks fine to me. Thanks."

Alicia stared at him for a minute. She made the nose huffing sound, then left.

Curtis waited until he heard the hum of the copy machine. He pulled open the desk drawer and took out his resume. He was re-reading the paragraph about his former employment then stopped, remembering a name he read on the list of attendees, Susie Nguyen. He had forgotten all about talking to her about the scholarship for the *Casa* children. The sisters, he was sure, would ask him about it. They'd find some way to corner him before or after the meeting, and he'd be forced to lie.

He placed the resume back in the drawer. He closed the drawer, rose, sat back down. Better lock the drawer. He didn't have proof Alicia looked through his desk when he was away, but there were times he opened drawers to find that files and papers were not how he had left them. He opened the center drawer, pulled the small key from the box where he kept his paper clips, locked the drawer and slid the key into his pocket.

16

Rochelle

———— ◈ ————

Rochelle heard the bell over the shop door ring as she walked down the stairs from her apartment. She carried a plate with a toasted bacon and tomato sandwich. It was noon, and she was hoping for a few minutes without customers so she could eat her lunch.

"Coming," Rochelle said, as she rounded the corner. Her visitor was Alicia, the secretary from the community center across the street.

"Hey, Alicia," Rochelle said. She sat the plate down and wiped her hands on a napkin.

"Good to see you again, Rochelle," Alicia said. She smiled and offered her hand. "I've been meaning to come over and see you. Make sure you were okay after what happened to Marcela. And your window." She looked at the new store front window. "I see you got the glass replaced. That's good."

Rochelle took Alicia's hand, grasping it with both of hers in a warm embrace. "I'm doing fine. The window's fixed, but it's going to take longer for our neighborhood to be repaired. Come, sit for a while. Would you like a BLT sandwich? I made myself one, won't take but a minute to fix you one."

"Sorry, not enough time today. Maybe next time. I'll be just a minute so you can get back to your lunch. If you recall, I called the other day to see if you were interested in helping at Marcela's vigil. We're having a planning meeting today, just those of us who are participating."

"Yes," said Rochelle. "I remember."

"Good. You're still coming, right? Since you're here all the time and the shop is busy, we thought you'd have some good input about the community."

Alicia talked more about the meeting and who was participating. Rochelle paid only half attention. Since you're here all the time, Alicia had said. It was true. The store was open ten hours during the week, and six hours on Saturday. Rochelle earned enough after paying the electric and gas bills, but there wasn't enough profit to justify hiring someone to help.

After she turned the sign around to show the shop was closed and locked the door, she went up the stairs to her one-bedroom apartment. Sometimes, she drove her Toyota Corolla to the store for groceries or to the mall so she could shop for clothes or something new for her home. On evenings when the weather was nice, she'd walk or ride the bicycle she stored in the back room. Mostly, Rochelle worked and waited. She waited for supplies for the shop to arrive, waited to open at eight in the morning and then to close at six in the evening, waited for Jim to call or come by.

"Here's a copy of the meeting agenda," Alicia said, the proffered sheet of paper jogging Rochelle from her contemplation.

"Thank you," Rochelle said, taking the paper. "I'll be there. And, Alicia," Rochelle continued, "let's go for lunch sometime, after things," she waved the agenda, "settle down. There's a new restaurant downtown that I've wanted to try."

Alicia's lips tightened for a moment, and Rochelle thought she was going to make up some excuse why she couldn't go. It would be an excuse that, although kind, would make it clear that Alicia's friendliness did not extend to their being friends outside the confines of the community center, or Rochelle's shop.

Alicia broke into a wide grin. "Let's do that," she said. "We both need to get away from this place for a little while,"

Alicia put her hand on Rochelle's arm, gave it a light squeeze. "See you at the meeting." The bell over the door gave a cheerful chime when Alicia left.

A few minutes before two o'clock, Rochelle wrote, "Will be back at 3:30" and taped the paper to the shop door. She locked the door behind her and walked across the street to the community center.

Rochelle looked around at the faces that circled the meeting room's large table. A few latecomers straggled in, pulling in chairs from other rooms and setting them against the wall. The room was crowded. A fan sat on the corner of a credenza, its head rotating back and forth to move cooler air over the heads of the attendees. Still, it felt claustrophobic. Rochelle recognized most of the people—the nuns from the mission and the priest from St. Guadalupe church and, of course, staff from the center. There were others she recognized from the panel at the public meeting. She didn't see Colonel Duc. That didn't surprise her.

Also absent, strange since the vigil was in celebration of her daughter's life, was Marcela's mother, Lucia. Antonio wasn't there either, but that didn't surprise Rochelle. There were townsfolk who believed that Antonio was the instigator, the hot spark that had ignited the firestorm that ended with his sister's death. Rochelle didn't believe Antonio was the spark, but just one component in the combustible fuel for the hot storm that had scorched her neighborhood.

Rochelle recalled how Lucia had been when she came into her shop after Marcela died. She'd been close to combusting too. Lucia was the snarling momma bear, angry at the loss of the one cub in which she stockpiled her future.

Curtis cleared his throat, tapping the microphone in front of him. The microphone whined and everyone winced. "Looks like everyone's here. Shall we start?"

Rochelle looked at Curtis. The hair at his temples was damp from sweat and his hand trembled slightly as he held a paper in his hand. He straightened his shoulders and he smiled.

"I'm glad to see everyone made it. I appreciate you all coming."

He glanced at the people seated at the table, making eye contact to acknowledge each. Curtis focused on Rochelle, held her eyes for a minute before moving on. Before he moved to the next person, Rochelle saw the desire for approval bloom in his eyes. He was trying, in his own way. Curtis didn't have the same easygoing sociability that Mark Kline had, but he had come far from the needy little man who visited her after the killing.

Rochelle read the paper Alicia handed out. The schedule had the vigil starting next Wednesday at six in the evening. There would be evocations made by Father Frank, the priest from St. Guadalupe Church, Father Trân from the predominately Vietnamese Catholic Church, and a Buddhist monk who was coming from a Wichita temple. His name wasn't listed. She listened as they discussed who would go first and whether to put time limits on the evocations.

Checking her watch, Rochelle found it had taken ten minutes just to decide which religious leader would go first and how long each should talk. Finally, all agreed that Father Frank from St. Guadalupe's would be the first speaker, since this was the church Marcela and her family attended.

After that subject was thoroughly analyzed, Chief of Police McKinley took the floor and said, "As I'm sure you're aware, there is a potential at the vigil for some type of retaliation. We're going to make sure that doesn't happen. By we, I mean Sheriff Folsom and our respective departments."

Rochelle stifled a yawn.

McKinley went on, "We plan to have both uniformed and plain-clothes officers present to keep the participants safe. We ask you," he swept the room to include all present, "to report any problems you encounter both at the vigil and during the preparations. The community's eyes are just as effective in preventing crime as an officer in the street." He paused for a minute as if the message needed time to permeate the crowd. "Thanks, Curtis," he said, and returned to his seat.

Next, three middle-aged ladies gave an accounting of the menu and drinks. Rochelle watched the participants talk. Marcela had been mentioned early in the meeting, but she seemed to have been forgotten as plans were forged.

"It looks like we've covered everything," said Curtis after the three ladies finished. "Is there anything we missed?"

Rochelle saw Chief McKinley impatiently check his watch. He fidgeted, anxious to get back to work. The ladies in charge of food and drink had their heads together, discussing what needed to be done.

Rochelle turned toward Curtis and raised her hand. Bracelets slid down her arm, clanking when they bumped against each other. Curtis turned toward the sound and beamed when he saw Rochelle's arm raised.

"Yes, Ms. Sanchez. You have a question?" asked Curtis.

Rochelle wondered at the formality of Curtis addressing her by her last name. He had called her Rochelle when he came over with the invitation of lunch. Was he trying to distance himself from her rejection, or was it for appearance, the show of paying respect to her position as shop owner and business neighbor. She couldn't recall how he had addressed the other speakers.

"I noticed Lucia Gomez, Marcela's mother, isn't here," Rochelle said. "She is going to participate, right?"

The room went quiet. Chief McKinley stopped fidgeting and cleared his throat. Eyes first sought Rochelle, bounced to Chief McKinley at the sound of his throat clearing, and landed on Curtis.

"Well, I…" Curtis began, "I mean, we decided. She, umm. Well, Chief?" There was almost plea in his voice when he addressed Chief McKinley.

All eyes rotated back to the police chief.

"We, or I, haven't directly talked to Mrs. Gomez. Of course, I'm sure she knows about the vigil."

He looked at Curtis. Curtis turned to look at Alicia. Alicia nodded.

"Of course, she's invited," the chief continued. "But this," he waved in the direction of the street outside, "has been extremely traumatic for her. You understand. We wouldn't want to put her on the spot, make things uncomfortable, you know."

Rochelle wondered just who would be uncomfortable. Someone to her left whispered and she caught the name Antonio.

"And there are security concerns with Antonio," said Curtis, wadding into the tension.

"That too," agreed the chief.

"Okay. Well, any other questions?" asked Curtis jumping up. "If not, we'll adjourn. Thank you all for coming. Why don't we meet again, briefly, next Tuesday afternoon, just to make sure everything's on track."

Dismissed, the attendees left. Curtis and Chief McKinley left together, quietly talking. The rest seemed to avoid Rochelle, walking cautiously around her, as if her invocation of Lucia's name was a jinx. Only Alicia caught Rochelle's eye and nodded.

The attendees lingered in the cool hallway talking or shaking hands. This might work. Rochelle had been doubtful, especially with Lucia's exclusion, but now, watching groups of people talk, she sensed their enthusiasm. No matter their different backgrounds, no matter that Kingston's residents would probably retreat to old habits and prejudices afterward, for a few hours everyone could come together with plans and hopes for an improved future.

Rochelle was busy the rest of the afternoon. Many of the people who had attended the meeting stayed around to visit her shop. She sold several summer shirts and some earrings that had lain for months inside the display box. Several customers eyed the bank of oak drawers and asked general questions about the contents. Rochelle suspected they would be back in a few days, when the shop was empty of customers, and they could talk to her in private.

It was six-thirty before the last customer left. Rochelle turned the sign around and locked the door. She climbed the stairs to her apartment, poured a glass of wine, and sat at the kitchen table to watch the last of the evening news. The long shadow from the building behind her made the apartment feel gloomy. She turned on lights and was preparing supper when Jim called.

"You're home, I see," Jim said, after Rochelle picked up the phone and said hello.

"Yes, I'm home, just getting ready to fix some broiled chicken for supper." She wondered if Jim watched her apartment and waited until he saw lights come on upstairs before calling. Was he worried about her, or just keeping track of her?

"Yummy. Mind if I come up for a while?"

"Sure, baby, I'm starving," Rochelle said, first a purr in her voice, then changing it to a mocking tone, "for supper. It's been a long day. Want to join me for something to eat and then, maybe," her tone turned back to the purr, "we can figure out desert."

"Hmm," Jim said, "are you talking about ice cream or did you bake up a sweet apple pie just for me."

"Yeah, right, apple pie, and then there goes my girlish figure. Come on up, we'll try and find something less fattening."

"We had the first appearance in court today for Truong Van Duc. He goes by Tommy. There was a second Vietnamese boy charged with murder too. A third boy was there when Marcela was shot, but he's only fifteen so there's a hearing scheduled to see if they're going to charge him as an adult or juvenile."

Jim spoke between bites of roasted chicken and a salad with fresh tomatoes and cucumber slices. Rachell made instant mashed potatoes the way Jim liked them with sour cream mixed into the potatoes and melted butter spread across on the top. She took tiny bites of the potatoes, savoring the rare treat.

"Are the two older boys in jail, or did they bond out?" asked Rochelle.

"Nope, the judge set their bonds at a quarter million. I doubt the families will be able to raise that much."

"And the fifteen year old. Is he still being held?"

"Nope," Jim said, "He has been released to his parents, pending charges."

"What?" said Rochelle. "Murder—and we're trusting his parents to keep an eye on him?"

"That's not the worse," Jim said. He put down his fork, looking intently at Rochelle. "What worries me are the three thugs who sat behind the defendants in the court room and glared at the judge and district attorney. It doesn't take a genius to figure out who our main witness in the case will be." He pointed his fork at Rochelle. "And I'm worried about that witness."

They were quiet for the rest of the dinner. Rochelle watched Jim. He had a tense look on his face and she wondered what he was thinking.

Jim carried his plate to the sink and then stood behind her. Pushing her hair to one side he kissed her neck then moved to her ear. Jim's tongue flicked the sensitive skin behind the ear and Rochelle's breath caught. She sat unmoving, enjoying the touch of his lips and tongue until she could no longer hold back the desire. Only then did she turn in the chair and wrap her arms around his waist.

"How did the planning meeting go?" asked Jim, much later after supper and a round of lovemaking. They were naked, sitting propped against the bed's headboard eating ice cream.

"It went okay. I was skeptical at first, but I think it will be a good opportunity for everyone to come together and work as a team."

"It's a start," said Jim. "But it won't help what's going on, underground, with the criminal activity. We have to weed out the criminal element or this 'community come-together' won't work."

"Sure, I know that. But, that's your job." Rochelle took her spoon, cold from the ice cream, and pressed it against Jim's bare chest to emphasize the point.

"Brrr, that's cold," he said laughing. Here, let me show you how cold. Rochelle tried to squirm away, but Jim grabbed her arm and pressed her bowl, still filled with ice cream, against her breast.

Rochelle took a shower after Jim left. Naked, she walked through the dark apartment and opened windows so a breeze could blow through, front to back. Late August days were hot in the dry, high plains, but like any desert climate, after the sun went down the dry air quickly cooled.

Rochelle had just opened the front window and pushed back the curtains when she heard music and felt a base beat. She stepped aside to observe the street but not be seen.

The music and bass beat became louder and she saw a car turn the corner onto Abilene Street. Suddenly, the music ended, and the car's lights went out. The car slowed, then stopped in front of her shop. Rochelle recognized the vehicle. It was the same one that had come down the cross street after the public met at the community center. Only a handful of people knew she lived above the shop, and the stairs up to her rooms from the shop were hidden behind a wall.

The street was eerily still, no sound or movement came from inside the car's dark interior. The backseat passenger stuck an arm out the open window. A finger extended from the fist like the barrel of a gun. He pointed it at her shop. Then the hand jerked up, like a gun does when fired. The arm jerked back inside, and tires screeched as it sped down the street.

Rochelle stood watch at the window for a long time, a breeze making the sheer curtain slip around her nude body. It wasn't until her heartbeat returned to normal and she quit shaking that she returned to the bedroom.

17

Curtis

————⬦————

Curtis stood when the sergeant entered. The officer filled the small office with his thick shoulders and wide leather belt with a pistol on one side and night stick on the other. His eyes bored through the fort Curtis had constructed on his side of the space with his desk, the inbox and a rack of file holders. Curtis stood not so much out of respect, but because the sergeant seemed to consume the room's meager oxygen, and he couldn't catch his breath.

"Sergeant Nicholas, isn't it?" asked Curtis. He wasn't sure why the officer was here. Alicia had poked her head in the door and announced the police wanted to see him. Curtis had been surprised, and he caught the smug look on Alicia's face when she told him they wanted to talk to him. She probably hoped they were here because he had done something wrong. Curtis wondered the same thing. He went through a mental list in his head: did he have an unpaid traffic ticket, or had something happened to Amy or Melody? The police, Alicia told him, making the word plural, but only one officer appeared.

"Curtis," acknowledged the officer. He looked around, his eyes settling first on Curtis' fortress and then on Alicia's metal table in the opposite corner. When he turned to face Curtis, his face was composed in a bland mask with no hint of what he was thinking.

"What brings you here today?" asked Curtis, anxious to break the silence. He and the sergeant had remained standing. Alicia came in and took her seat, the chair emitting a faint squeak. The officer turned to face her and said, "Morning, Alicia."

Alicia appeared surprised, as if she had been so occupied with her work that she didn't realize Sgt. Nicholas was still there. Curtis knew better.

"Sergeant Nicholas, good to see you again," Alicia said with a bright smile. "Better circumstances this time, I hope."

"Let's go to the conference room," said Curtis, stepping out from behind his fortification. He didn't know, yet, what the officer wanted. What he did know was that he didn't want Alicia's inquisitive ears in the room.

Curtis attempted small talk as they walked down the hall to the conference room. He was still going through the mental list in his head. When did his car tags expire? His driver's license? Amy had always reminded him of these things and couldn't recall. Had someone filed a complaint about the center? Was this about Melody or Amy? The officer didn't look tense, that probably meant Amy and Melody were okay.

The officer's question stilled the list crafting.

"When we talked after the shooting," Sgt. Nicholas said, "you indicated the Center was putting in security cameras. I looked this morning, but couldn't find any visible, either over the front or side doors. Were they installed?"

Curtis recalled talking about a camera, but it had slipped his mind with all the other things that had happened after. He searched for an answer, found one.

"I have to discuss it with the board first. Something like a camera, it's costly, so I'd have to get their approval first. Why do you ask?"

"We got a report of activity last night in the street outside the community center. Thought if the incident was recorded, we could identify who was involved."

"Incident?" Curtis asked. "Everything looked okay when I came in this morning."

"Right. There wasn't damage, but someone in a car threatened a witness to the shooting."

"What time? Someone here at the center?

"No. It happened late last night. Not a witness at the center."

Who was it, then? Curtis tried to recall the afternoon Marcela was killed. He had seen officers talk to the lady who owned the sewing repair place across the street. He didn't know the owner's name. Lights were usually on in her store when Curtis arrived in the morning and, occasionally, in the afternoon when she walked across the street to the old van she parked in the Center's lot. Then there was Rochelle's shop directly across the street.

"Was it Rochelle?" Curtis asked. His throat had tightened, and it came out squeaky.

Sergeant Nicholas nodded. "We don't want this information out, you understand. She lives in an apartment over the shop. They stopped in the street last night and made threatening gestures. They may not have realized she was there, but we're not taking chances. She's our best witness, wouldn't want something to happen to her."

Nicholas' arm rested on the table and Curtis noticed that his hand had curled into a fist. His expression was neutral, but the fist was a tell. He recalled seeing the sergeant help Rochelle board up the broken shop window. Were they friends or something more? He didn't see a wedding ring on the officer's left hand. Not that it meant anything, not anymore.

"Oh, I didn't know she lived upstairs."

"Yeah," the sergeant said. "Like I said, we don't want that known."

"Well, I'll definitely keep an eye out for any problems. I'll make sure she stays safe," Images flashed in his mind: Rochelle calling for help and Curtis rushing across the street, guns blazing at masked men dressed in black.

The officer's fist relaxed, and Curtis saw the corner of his mouth twitch up in a smile.

"We appreciate that, but I suspect a security camera is more helpful." He paused. "A camera can keep watch all night. You're not here at night, are you?"

"Well, no but…."

The sergeant said nothing. His eyes were cool ice, but his mouth once again twitched as if he could read Curtis' thoughts and found them amusing.

The daydream of riding to Rochelle's rescue dissolved.

"Okay," he said. "I'll bring it up to the board. See if I can convince them to purchase a couple of cameras."

Curtis thought about his conversation with Nicholas as he drove to his old home to pick up Melody. He always thought of the house where he and Amy had lived as home, not the apartment where he lived now, with the kitchen cupboard doors that refused to close tight no matter how hard or soft he shut the doors, and the dingy beige carpet installed because it camouflaged grim tracked in by the string of renters who had inhabited the space.

There was some odd connection between Rochelle and the police officer, something that hinted of familiarity, but also detachment. He wondered if Rochelle had given Nicholas, with his sharp eyes and tense beefy body, the same brush off that she had given to Curtis. That must be it, he decided. Curtis told Nicholas that he would drive by Rochelle's later after he dropped off his daughter, but the officer had looked hard at Curtis and told him not to worry.

"We're watching out for her," Nicholas had said, and Curtis, seeing finality in the muscle that twitched in the officer's check, had nodded his assent.

Curtis loved taking Melody to purchase her school supplies. This had been their special time together ever since Melody began kindergarten. He walked down the aisles of school supplies alongside his daughter with the same happy expectation that he had felt as a student. There was something about the orderly displays of notebook paper, new pencils and pens, and erasers and rulers that invited optimism for the new school year. Curtis had done well in grade school, at least in math and science, and late summer beckoned to him like a New Year's Eve resolution. Each fall, he'd pledge to work hard, make all As this school year. He'd keep the storage compartment under the desktop neatly arranged and his pencils sharpened to fine points. This year, he'd make friends who would appreciate him for his intellect and precise manner. This new year, he would no longer be the clumsy boy who was always chosen last for schoolyard games of soccer and baseball.

"So, you're in third grade this year?" teased Curtis, reading the list of required school supplies taped to the support post in the K-Mart aisle.

"No, Dad. I'm in fourth grade. Don't you remember?" She glared at her dad, hands on hips, in mock admonishment.

Curtis slapped his forehead with the heel of his hand. "Fourth grade. I can't believe it. Are you sure?"

"Oh, Dad. I'm almost ten, you know. I'm in fourth grade." The last sentence Melody said slowly and distinctly as if talking to a feeble-minded adult.

"Okay, if you say so. Looks like you'll need all this," Curtis said, pointing to the list, "plus a calculator. Guess we'd better get started."

They walked down one aisle and then the next picking up notebook paper, yellow pencils, and a package of blue pens.

"Here's a notebook with a Cabbage Patch Kid on it," Curtis said looking at the selection of red, blue, green, and yellow notebooks. "Didn't you have one like this last year?"

"I like this one better," said Melody. She held up a notebook with a graphic of E.T. "We saw the movie, remember. E.T. phone home," she said in a low gravelly voice and then laughed. Curtis had a sudden memory of Marcela in his office saying the same phrase in the same gravelly voice. He cleared his throat, took a handkerchief from his trouser pocket, and blew his nose. No, he was not going to invite the little girl's ghost into this happy occasion with Melody.

"All right, put it in the cart then," Curtis said, using the same gravelly voice, and pointing to the cart, one finger extended in parody of the alien's gesture.

Another customer, two sons in tow, turned and smiled at them. Other shoppers paid them no attention. They were busy with their own children, a chorus of "Mom," and "I need," and "I want" sounding through the crowded aisle.

Curtis wound their cart through the busy store and to the checkout. Finally, they were out of the store and into the warm summer evening. Was it his imagination or were the days already shorter as Earth once again tilted toward fall.

He drove Melody back to her mother's house. His daughter talked animatedly about her summer swimming classes, new friends in the neighborhood, and the movie she and her mom saw last week. Finally talked out, she lapsed into silence.

"Your mom told me she'd think about you going to the vigil with me. She said anything to you about it?"

"I heard her talking to Mike" she started to say, and then looked quickly at her dad when she realized that the name of her mom's new boyfriend had intruded into the car. "Mike stays all night with mom," she said quietly, more to herself than her dad. "I don't like it when he stays with us."

Curtis stopped for a red signal light and asked his daughter, "You told Mom that?"

"I did," Melody said. She was picking at her fingernails, pulling the cuticle away from the nail bed. Curtis noticed her cuticles were red. When had this nervous habit started?

The light turned green, and Curtis focused on the road. When he and

Amy separated, he'd purchased a book on what to say to children about divorce. He tried to remember the advice it gave on what to say to a child when a new boyfriend or girlfriend moves in with the ex-spouse. He couldn't recall.

There was something in the book he did remember. "Melody, has Mike done anything to make you feel uncomfortable?" Mike liked to tell off-color stores when they played golf, back when he and Amy were still married and Mike had been his friend, not Amy's. He'd kill Mike if he ever touched his daughter. Curtis realized his knuckles were white where they gripped the steering wheel. He forced himself to relax, tried to compose his face into a one that showed concern and not anger. He turned to Melody, cocked an eyebrow in question.

"No, Dad, not that," Melody said, worrying her cuticles again. "Mom had the talk with me about bad touch and we talk about it in school too." She said it in a long sigh like it was a subject she was tired of hearing.

Curtis forced himself to take a deep breath, relax.

"So, back to what we were talking about earlier. Did Mom decide if you can go with me?"

"I think she's going to let me go," his daughter said, and in the deft way she always had of changing an unpleasant subject said, "Hey, Dad, look, there's the Dairy Queen. Please, please, can we stop for ice cream?"

18

Rochelle

———◇———

Rochelle inhaled fresh morning air as she walked through the cemetery to Angelina's grave. It was a little after seven o'clock and the air was scented with freshly-mowed grass and damp earth. The new day's sun filtered through the leaves of the elm trees and dappled the shade. Rochelle sniffed the bouquet of gold and brown sunflowers and burgundy chrysanthemums. They had little smell. The hot house flowers were grown for their appearance, rather than fragrance. She pulled down the wrapper to expose the bouquet. The crackle of cellophane was loud in the quiet morning. Rochelle squatted and laid the flowers in front of Angelina's gray granite headstone.

Rochelle missed her *abuela*, wished she was still here so she could talk to her about dangerous boys who made threats with hands held like pistols. Having risked migration from Puerto Rico for a better life, Angelina could offer advice.

What Rochelle needed was a vacation, time away from the sameness of each day. She normally closed the shop the week between Christmas and the New Year and traveled to Miami, or some other location where days were warm and sunny, but Christmas was months away.

Last night, she opened the road atlas to the map of the United States. Placing a finger on Kingston in the middle of the map, she traced the interstates going east and west, then to the north and south, unsure which direction she wanted to travel. Maybe, it was because there were too many destinations possible from Kansas, this state in the middle of the country. When she lived in Miami, her choices were west or north, but here there were too many. Rochelle closed the atlas and put it away.

What she needed was a respite from the gangs, Jim's indecision, and her loneliness here where the flat land and wide sky felt oddly claustrophobic. Or was the restlessness a portent that it was time to move on—have the surgery so she could leave behind this place with its baggage of her painful childhood.

"I miss you so much, *Abuela*," she said. She put fingertips to her pursed lips and pressed the kiss to Angelina Maria Trujillo Sanchez's name carved into the granite face of the stone.

Mid-morning, Rochelle watched Alicia walk across the street to her shop. Alicia pushed the door open, the vigilant bell above the door announcing the visitor. Rochelle was glad for the company. She had little business the last couple of days. Customers who earlier bought summer merchandise as way to ward off the end of summer had turned to other pursuits anticipating the start of school and time constructs that called for curfews and a ten o'clock bedtime.

"Would you like to help us with the candles?" Alicia asked, after a several minutes of small talk.

Rochelle's curiosity had grown as they discussed the start of school and the lingering hot weather that threatened to cut short the first days of school in the non-air-conditioned classrooms. Alicia was normally direct and organized, not one to dally with talk of the weather.

"Sure," said Rochelle. "It'll be a welcome break from this slow day."

"That's great," said Alicia.

Rochelle agreement seemed to have vanquished some of Alicia's tension but there was more to it judging by the nervous way the assistant toyed with her hair.

"Well, I," Alicia started, "well, Curtis asked me to ask you to help."

"That's fine. I said in the meeting that I was willing to help in any way."

Alicia sighed loudly. "I mean, he wanted me to tell you the request came from him. Him, personally."

Rochelle tilted her head back and laughed. "Oh, I see it now. You can report back to the boss that the message was received."

Alicia shrugged. "I think he has a crush on you. He watches you with those moony eyes. It's embarrassing."

"Not as embarrassing as him finding out I didn't originally come with these," Rochelle said, cupping a hand under each breast and bouncing them.

"Oh, God," said Alicia, laughing and blushing. "That would be something to watch. I'd never be able to look him in the eyes again without cracking up."

"Me, too, girl," said Rochelle.

Before she went across the street to help Alicia, Rochelle pulled off the barrette that clasped her hair in a ponytail at her neck and brushed out the hair. She had no interest in Curtis, but it was fun to tease.

His awkwardness when she greeted him was transparent in the blush that bloomed from beneath his collar. This petty ploy to tease Curtis was another sign she needed a vacation.

"I'll show you what we're doing," Alicia told Rochelle. When they were settled in the Center's conference room. Boxes of white candles sat on the table alongside plastic bags of three-ounce, waxed Dixie cups.

Alicia picked up a thin blade, more a scalpel than a knife, and slit a small "X" into the bottom of one of the cups. She pushed the tip of a candle up through the cup bottom to the middle of the candlestick. Alicia held up it.

"See, the cup catches the hot wax from the candle, keeps it from dripping onto people's hands." She motioned to the boxes of candles. "We have three hundred to do. We'll pass them out to the attendees. They'll be lighted during the prayers, and we'll keep them lit as we walk from the center to the park. I wish we could get the city to turn the streetlights off, make the candlelight really show, but Chief McKinley nixed that idea. He said his officers won't be able to monitor the crowd in the dark."

Rochelle had been opening the plastic bags that held the cups, but now she looked at Alicia.

"The Chief thinks there'll be trouble at the vigil?" She remembered the boys in the car outside her window.

"No, no," said Alicia, waving the thought away. "There'll be lots of officers there to watch. We'll be fine."

Rochelle wasn't so sure. Several times she had called Lucia, Marcela and Antonio's mother, but no one answered the phone. Jim told her they were keeping tabs on Antonio and his friends, as well as members of the Dragon Boyz, the Vietnamese gang allegedly responsible for Marcella's death. He said they were monitoring the different factions, Jim's words, but refused to give details when Rochelle asked. She had tried to tug the information from him by acting coy, running a painted fingernail down his chest, but Jim just smiled at her and said, "Don't worry, babe, I'm watching out for you."

"I'll be back in a minute," Alicia said, pulling Rochelle's thoughts back to the room and the cups. "Gotta make a couple of calls, check on some things, then I'll be back to help."

Rochelle examined the blade, turning it so light from the overhead florescent bulbs bounced off its surface. She was half-way through the second package of Dixie cups when Curtis stuck his head in the conference room door. He smiled and asked how they were doing. For a minute, she thought the rest of his body would follow the grin into the room. But Curtis just gave her a little finger wave and moved on down the hall. Rochelle figured he would soon be back, but ten minutes passed before he stuck his head in again.

"Looks like you've made good headway," Curtis said. He entered the room and laid a manila file folder on the table, but didn't pull out a chair to sit. She suspected he was waiting for an invitation to join her. It was ironic that he felt he needed permission to sit in his own conference room. She waved a hand at the chair.

"Six dozen done, but still a ways to go," she said, putting the blade down and wiggling her fingers to loosen the tightness caused by gripping the blade.

"I'm glad you offered to help," Curtis said. She waited him to say something more, but he didn't.

"Thanks. Do you know how many people are coming?"

The awkward conversation went on a little longer, Rochelle asking unimportant questions just to fill the silence. Finally, Curtis leaned forward, tapped the file folder.

"There hasn't been anything official said, yet, but thought you'd be interested to know that since Dr. Kline is retiring, they're looking to fill his position. I've been told I have a good chance at being named the new director."

He stopped speaking, a puppy-like need for approval on his face.

"That's good news. Congratulations, Curtis. They'll announce it soon?"

A shadow passed over Curtis' face. He flushed.

"Well, I don't believe the board is that far along and, please," he leaned forward and his voice dropped to a whisper, "don't tell anyone yet. I mean, since you own the shop across the street and we might work together in the future, I thought you should know."

Rochelle smiled. "My lips are zipped." She drew her hand across her mouth, as if zipping her lips closed.

"Oh, thanks," Curtis said, visible relieved.

Mmmmph, Rochelle said, talking through zippered lips.

Curtis laughed, and the longing in his eyes almost made Rochelle regret the little flirt that offered a morsel of hope to this lonely man. She would have recognized his loneliness, even without the knowledge she had acquired through the neighborhood grapevine about the loss of his old job and the divorce.

Curtis picked up the file. "Better get back to work. Need to make a good impression, you know." He winked at Rochelle.

Alicia had twice walked past the room while Curtis and Rochelle talked. The first time, Rochelle looked up to see Alicia pause and lift her eyebrows. Rochelle quickly looked away, afraid that Curtis would catch the suppressed amusement. The second time, Rochelle heard the click of Alicia's heels on the linoleum, but didn't look up. She entered, carrying two Tupperware glasses.

"Thought you'd like something cold to drink," Alicia said, setting the glasses on the table. "It's sweet iced tea. Instant, but still good."

"Thank you," said Rochelle. She took a sip and set the glass on the table. Curtis extended a hand toward Alicia, anticipating she would hand him the second glass. Alicia ignored him, took a long swallow of the tea, set the glass on the table, pulled out a chair and sat down.

Curtis glared at Alicia for a moment. Then he turned to Rochelle and said, "Later."

Alicia and Rochelle talked as they worked on the candles. Finally, they were done and the cups, each with an "X" cut into the bottom were stacked neatly on the table. Next to them were the white, wax candles, still in their boxes.

"Tomorrow, we'll pass out the cups and candles and let everyone put them together. Easier to store that way."

Alicia walked Rochelle to lobby. "See you tomorrow?"

"Of course," replied Rochelle. The vigil begins at six p.m. I'll come over between three and four to help get ready."

It was almost five o'clock by the time Rochelle unlocked the shop door and flipped the sign over to show the shop was once again open. Only one customer came in. She looked at the displays and fingered the price tags, but didn't purchase anything. The customer gave Rochelle a cheery goodbye when she left, the bell over the door ringing out its farewell. Rochelle straightened shirts on the rack and dusted the countertops, trying to hasten time before she gave up and closed the shop ten minutes early.

She climbed the back steps to her apartment, flexing her fingers as she went up. She used her hands making jewelry, but holding the slender knife and the repetitive movement had made her fingers stiff. The apartment was hot, and Rochelle turned the window air conditioner to high. She was debating whether to ride her bicycle or take a long bath and try the new bath oil she ordered for the shop when the phone rang.

"Hello."

"Hey, babe," said Jim, in the soft low voice he always used when he called. "Are you closed yet?"

"Yeah," Rochelle said. "Business was slow so I shut down early."

"What are you doing now?"

"Just deciding whether I want to take a long bath or a bicycle ride. Why?" It was unusual for Jim to call this early. He worked long hours and, normally, didn't call on her until dark, when he could slip unnoticed through the shop's back door and up the stairs.

"Aren't you at work?" she asked. She envisioned Jim at the police station huddled over the phone so no one overheard their conversation. For not the first time, she wished things were different or they lived some place where they didn't have to hide their conversations from co-workers.

"No, I'm at the payphone at the Kwik Shop. Ride your bike down to the high school. Meet me in the parking lot. I have something to show you."

"What?"

"Some photos. We have a lead on the boys who have been driving by your shop. I need you to identify them."

"Last time I just came to the station. Why the clandestine meet in the parking lot?"

She heard Jim take a deep breath.

"I thought I'd run by McDonald's. Pick up a couple of burgers and then we could sit at the picnic tables outside the high school, look at the photos and eat."

Rochelle's heart sang.

"You mean out in public and everything?" The words were mocking, but her tone was kind.

"It's shady and quiet there and I thought. Well, I just thought, you know."

"Let me change into some shorts and pull the bike out. I'll be there in less than thirty minutes." Rochelle's voice became even softer. "I care about you, you know."

"Yep, same here," he said, and disconnected the call.

Rochelle sat beside Jim at the round concrete picnic table in the shaded area between the high school and the football stadium. She sneaked a fry off the neatly-folded wrapper under Jim's cheeseburger. It was crispy with a fluffy potato center. Rochelle took a tiny bite, then another, as she studied the photos Jim laid in front of her.

"I can't tell," Rochelle said, tapping a photo with the nub of the French fry. "The streetlight was out on the corner, and I was looking down from the second floor. The driver wore a baseball cap, so I didn't even see his face. The one who mimed shooting at the shop never stuck his head out the back window. The face was a white oval with no discernable features. Now the car, I did see that. It was either a Toyota or Datsun, something small and sporty, with a hatchback."

"Older model or late model?"

Rochelle tapped a finger against her lips, thought. "Hard to say, hatchback all I know for sure. Two-door, but the passenger was in the back seat. That rules out a Datsun 280Z. They don't have a back seat."

"A Datsun 160J or Violet model, maybe?" asked Jim.

Rochelle brushed a strand of hair off her cheek. "I'm not familiar with those. My guess is a Toyota Celica, something like that."

"There're a couple of different Celica body styles," Jim said. He pushed around the salt he had sprinkled on the French fries. "The Celica GT and a Supra models have the hatchback. Did the headlights flip up?"

"Let me think," said Rochelle. She thought back to that night, seeing the car stop in the street and the headlights wink out. "Yes, they did flip. I noticed the light swept up when they came back on."

"Good. That narrows it down. A Toyota Celica Supra has that kind of headlights."

Rochelle remembered something else. "Oh, yeah, and the car had nice rims. Not a solid hubcap but a cut design."

"Supra," Jim said. Did you see the color?

"Couldn't tell for sure. It was night and the car was dark. I'd guess black or blue."

"Not a pale blue?" said Jim.

"No, darker. It may have even been red. Red looks dark at night."

Jim took a bite of his sandwich and chewed slowly. He gazed into the distance, his elbows resting on the concrete table. Rochelle took the opportunity to sneak another French fry.

"What you said helps," Jim said, "Couple of cars like that belong to people we're watching." He took a drink, turned back to Rochelle, "Folks on both sides of the dispute."

Jim's blue eyes pinned her, like they had the first time they met. His eyes were the color of Blue Jay feathers, or the blue in photos she had seen of Arctic icebergs. But these eyes weren't cold like glacial ice, but warm and concerned. He laid a hand on top of hers making her insides flood with sudden heat.

"We'll figure it out," Jim said, and Rochelle wasn't sure if he meant the two of them, or the car's occupants.

19

Curtis

———⬦———

It was almost 10 o'clock before Curtis arrived at work the day of the vigil. He'd gone early to the *Casa de la Gente* hopping to catch the nuns before they became busy. What he found, at seven thirty in the morning, was Sister Beatrice already busy with her day and Sister Clarice called away for something the girl at the front desk declined to say. He sat on the same hard bench in the lobby for 10 minutes. Finally, the receptionist walked Curtis down the hall to the nun's office.

"Thank you for coming by," Sister Beatrice said, taking his proffered hand in both of her large, bony ones. "How are things progressing for this evening's activities? You must be very busy. I apologize for making you wait." She waved him to a chair and sat opposite him.

"Not a problem," said Curtis. "We're busy, sure, but I wanted to let you know the board has agreed to offer two childcare scholarships."

Curtis had brought up the subject at the board meeting expecting they would reject it, but was surprised when, not only had they approved it, they also praised him for proposing the scholarship idea. Initially, Curtis told them it had been the nuns' suggestion, but when he saw their heads nidding in agreement, he reshaped the proposal, moving the credit in front of him like chips in a poker game. It was true, after all. Hadn't he had been the one who brought it up to Susie, convinced her it was good for both the Center and the town?

"It's economics and lack of a family support structure that bring the poor to the mission, not necessarily any flaw in their character," he told Susie, echoing what Sister Clarice said. "Who knows, maybe one of the kids will grow up and cure cancer or become president," he added, this time using his own words. Susie was reluctant at first but warmed to the idea. They would make room for the children without too much extra cost, but no more than two, she had told Curtis, and only after school starts and they had fewer to manage. That, too, he had relayed to the board members sitting around the Center's conference table. "Only two, and not until September after school begins. The only cost we'll incur will be for extra food for the kids. For everything else we can use existing resources."

Curtis savored the memory of the nun's gratitude and the positive reaction from the board while he drove to work. Mark Kline had attended the directors' meeting. He looked even frailer than he did during the visit to his house. His shaky steps into the conference room were made with a weary economy. Curtis rolled in Kline's old office chair so he could sit in something more comfortable than the thinly-padded chairs around the conference room table. Kline had sunk gratefully into the soft cushions, his face white against the plush leather.

Curtis passed out the quarterly accounting of the center's income and expenses and updated the members on the progress of the grant application. What he didn't tell them was how long he'd spent on the phone with the Department of Human Health Services talking first with a receptionist, and then working up the Department's staff ladder until he found someone authorized to accept the late application. Yes, he had pleaded, he knew they were past the deadline, but there had been extraordinary circumstances with the shooting and the girl's death. Yes, he would send copies of the police report and newspaper articles. Of course, he was a witness, and the police demanded he stay and talk to them and write up his account. The part about his being a witness was somewhat exaggerated, he knew, but wasn't the result worth a little tugging at the truth. Finally, after he submitted police reports, his notarized statements, and clipped newspaper articles, they extended the deadline and approved the grant request.

After what seemed like endless questions about the account statement, grant application, operation of the center, and the daycare scholarship proposal, Curtis was thanked and then excused so the board members could discuss other matters. A couple of the members stood and stretched while Curtis gathered his papers and pens. Others visited or read the documents he had passed around. Mark Kline smiled at him. Curtis took it as a positive sign.

He tossed the extra documents on his desk, but didn't turn on the light. He didn't want to see the space where he had been regulated with its stuffy atmosphere and Alicia's desk perched awkwardly by the door. He walked down the hall to Kline's old office. This time, he did turn on the lights. His eyes lingered on the darkened window to the street and the wall shelves behind Kline's desk with their neatly arranged books and framed photos. Then, he flipped off the light, quietly pulled the door shut behind him, and exited through the staff door to the parking lot.

Curtis got in his car but didn't start it. What were the board members discussing in the conference room with the door shut so their voices wouldn't float into the hall? Did they have other applicants for the director position? He had been checking the newspaper classifieds every day to see if the director's position was posted, but no posting appeared. Did that mean they used other means of recruiting, or did it mean they had already decided to offer the directorship to him? It was hot in the car and Curtis rolled down the windows. He thought about staying to watch the board members leave and observe their reactions but decided it was not be a good idea. Pole lights illuminated the lot. The lights would reveal both his car and him lurking inside. It would be awkward, and hard to explain, if they came over to see if he was okay. Curtis started the engine and wound his way through the streets to his dark apartment.

"Where have you been?" asked Alicia when he strolled through the lobby. There were already tables set up in front of the entrance. Two teenage girls were busy wiping dust off the tops and legs. Alicia looked flustered. Strands of hair had escaped from the knot on the back of her head and lay in damp clumps on her neck. Her feet were bare. How many times had he told her to keep her shoes on and here she was, again, parading barefoot in front of their clients and visitors.

"I was on a work errand," said Curtis. What business was it of hers, anyway? He had a brief fantasy about handing Alicia a pink slip (in his fantasy it really was pink) and telling her she was being replaced by someone else, someone with a more agreeable personality. What he told her was, "The vigil doesn't start until six. We have plenty of time, no reasons for you to go flapping around," he flapped his arms like a chicken trying to avoid an axe wielded by a farmer's wife, "getting all worried about stuff. And where are your shoes? How many times have I told you, this is a public place. You must wear shoes. It's the law." His voice rose righteously on the last sentence.

"Oh, good God," snapped Alicia, hands on her hips. "We have a ton of things that need to be done before six, before then, really, since I know people will show up early. We have to get pitchers of ice water outside and chairs for the elderly and the pregnant. We need to get the stage set up and wired for the speakers and the mic, and…"

Curtis interrupted her. "And wasn't there some volunteer committee that was supposed to arrange everything? Maybe you forgot that you're a paid employee of this center and while you're on the clock you're supposed," he emphasized supposed, "to be doing center work, not this." Curtis waved his hand around. The two girls dusting the tables stopped what they were doing and watched the argument. They frowned at Curtis and scooted closer to Alicia, as if they had already selected sides in this dispute.

"Do what you have to do," said Curtis, worried about gossip making it back to the board and thwarting his chances. "At least put your shoes back on," he hissed. With that last directive delivered, Curtis strode to his office. The fantasy of handing Alicia a pink slip once again ran through his mind. He'd let her go immediately, not give her the opportunity to stay and train her replacement. How hard was her job, anyway? She answered the phone, sat at the receptionist desk, typed letters. Anyone could do it, and anyone would be more agreeable than this busy-body, self-appointed head of the Dr. Mark Kline fan club.

He tried to work on tonight's speech, but voices and the noise of tables and chairs being moved in the lobby interpreted his concentration. He impatiently tapped a pencil on the desktop and, finally, gave up. He'd offer to help and then leave early so he could eat a late lunch and pick up Melody.

When Roger Munoz appeared, Curtis was glad he had volunteered to set up an awning in the street. Roger owned an insurance agency. More importantly, he was one of the center's board members.

"Mr. Munoz, good to see you again," said Curtis. He was in the middle of threading one the awning's support poles through a pocket in the canvas top. He finished and wiped his hands on his trousers before extending a hand to him.

"Same here," Munoz said. "Please call me Roger. Looks like you have things under control."

"Yes," said Curtis. He considered the argument he had earlier with

Alicia and the potential for harmful gossip and said, "We've been lucky to have Alicia's assistance." He waved his hand toward Alicia. She looked up at the sound of her name, focusing first on Curtis and then on Roger.

"Good to see you, Roger," Alicia acknowledged.

She went back to what she was doing, ignoring Curtis.

Roger helped Curtis erect the awning. As he did, Curtis studied him, seeking any clue as to what the board members discussed after they excused Curtis and pulled the door shut. Munoz gave nothing away.

Anxious, but hesitant to ask directly, Curtis finally said, "Did the meeting go on long after I left?"

"Not long," Munoz said.

His answer was as revealing as his body language had been when he helped Curtis erect the tent. In other words, Curtis learned nothing.

"Well, that's done," Roger said. He took a bright, white handkerchief from his pocket and used it to scrub the dirt from his hands. He folded it into a square, but didn't push the dirty cloth back into his pocket.

Curtis grimaced. He didn't have a handkerchief, and he didn't want to wipe his hands on his pants again. He checked where the awning pole dug into the asphalt trying, inconspicuously, to see if the sides of his trousers were marked with dirt where he had previously wiped his hands.

As if he could read Curtis' mind, Roger hiked up a trouser leg and brushed off a bit of something Curtis couldn't see. Did the gesture indicate Roger's opinion of Curtis or was it just the unconscious gesture of a man who knew customers linked skill in recommending insurance to his appearance.

"I'll be back later," Roger said. "Hope to see you then, Curtis."

After Munoz left, Curtis checked at his watch. It showed one-thirty. As if on cue, his stomach growled. The morning had passed quickly. Chairs were lined in rows in the street and tables waited on the sidewalk. Black and white stripped blockades had been placed at each end of the block closing off the street between the center and the park. While Curtis and Roger set up the awing, a pickup parked a trailer with the stage. Now workers were stringing a red, white, and blue skirt around the bottom of the stage to hide the trailer's wheels.

"I'm going to pick up my daughter. Be back at later," Curtis told Alicia. He left before she could protest.

Melody was sitting on the porch swing when Curtis pulled into the driveway of Amy's house. The swing slowly swung back and forth. Melody was dressed in a cotton striped dress. A band of ribbon held the hair off her forehead. Behind the ribbon, curls blossomed. As he came close, Curtis saw Melody's head was down. She was twisting and untwisting the strap of a small purse that she held in her lap. One foot was tucked under her leg. The other foot pushed against the floor of the porch, making the swing move. She looked up and Curtis saw a worried expression in her eyes.

"What's wrong, baby?" he asked, sitting down beside her. "It looks like you're upset. You don't want to go?"

"No, I want to go."

The front door opened. Amy came out, said, "Oh, there you are. I wondered where you went."

Curtis felt Melody stiffen beside him. Amy's face was flushed, and her movements were hurried and jerky. He had lived with her long enough to be attuned to her emotions and the flushed face and awkward movements meant she was upset about something. She looked down the street, then turned her head to scan the other direction. Curtis didn't say anything, knowing from experience that any words from him would just exacerbate her bad mood.

Amy turned to her daughter and, as if seeing Curtis for the first time, said, "Oh, hi. Melody's been waiting for you."

"Amy," he said. He took Melody's hand and stood, giving Amy a smile he hoped was disarming. "Looks like we're ready to go."

"I want her back before her bedtime. I'm trying to get her used to going to bed early so she can wake up early. School starts next week, you know."

"Sure," Curtis said. He squeezed Melody's hand. "I'll have her back around nine or so."

"Eight-thirty," Amy said, putting fists on her hips. "Before that even. It's bad enough her being in that neighborhood. After dark it's worse, what with everything that goes on there. I can't understand why…"

Curtis interrupted before Amy could launch into her litany, "Nine or so. Remember, we already discussed it. And there'll be lots of people there. Police too. It's the safest place in the city tonight. We'll be fine." He smiled at Melody, trying to reassure her, but Melody was watching her mother, an intent look on her face.

"Well…" Amy started to say.

Curtis interrupted, "You know our daughter will be safe with me." He gently pressed Melody's shoulder, prompting her toward the porch steps.

Melody turned the radio on as soon as they got in the car and punched the pre-programmed button for her favorite station. Michael Jackson's *Billie Jean* filled the car, leaving little space for Melody and Curtis to talk. Curtis didn't say anything, just let the music wind through its melody and chorus, giving Melody time. He drove by a McDonald's. Pulling into the drive-up lane he turned down the volume.

"I had a late lunch, but do you want something? No telling when we'll eat tonight."

"Cheeseburger and orange soda, please," Melody whispered.

"Your mom upset about your going with me?" Curtis asked Melody after he placed their order and waited for their turn at the service window.

"It's not that," Melody said, twisting the strap of her purse.

"Is your mom upset with you?"

"No." Melody took a deep breath. "Mom had a big fight with Mike." She spit out his name like it was a bad taste in her mouth.

"Oh," Curtis said. He was curious, but hesitant to intrude into the confidences between Melody and her mother. Instead, he just let the friendless word dangle in the quiet car.

"He's such a dork," Melody finally said. "He comes over for supper every night." She rolled her eyes and then in her deep voice mimicked Mike, "You cook so good. I'd just have to eat TV dinners if I was home. Oh, can you rub my neck. Work makes me so tense." Melody rolled her shoulders in an imitation of enjoying a neck rub. "It's so gross."

Then Melody said. "I think dorky Mike has another girlfriend. That's what their fight was about. Some lady called our house, and he took the phone outside to talk. But Mom has caller ID." She said the last in a sing-song voice.

"Well, your Mom was always the smart one," Curtis said, keeping his voice neutral. Inside he cheered. When he took Melody home, he'd tell Amy the board was considering him for the center's director. Maybe, she'd invite him to sit on the porch swing and they'd talk. The dull light from the streetlamp down the block would provide the only illumination. If Mike was out of the picture, he and Amy could piece together a new relationship. He'd do things differently this time. Or, he'd entice Amy, let her know he was moving up in his job, but slip in that he was happy as a bachelor.

He'd be sitting in a restaurant with a beautiful woman beside him. They'd be holding hands, her head bent toward him, listening attentively. Then he'd glance up and see Mike and Amy walk in. They'd walk in together, but there would be a coldness between them. They would survey the restaurant, but they wouldn't say anything to each other. Then Amy would spot Curtis beside his date. He'd ignore her. Or, maybe, he'd introduce his beautiful date to Amy and Mike and watch the jealously flicker in his ex-wife's eyes.

"Dad," said Melody, intruding on his daydream, "you can move up now."

Curtis found the parking lot full when they arrived back at the Center.

"Damn," he said when he found an older model Oldsmobile in the spot where he usually parked. Worse, the car was parked askew, with a front tire sitting on the line and the rear intruding into the next stall. He thought he could squeeze his car in beside the Oldsmobile, but he was afraid whoever had rudely taken his parking place would scrape down the side of his car when they pulled out. Instead, he and Melody drove through the lot, down one street and up another until he found an empty space.

Curtis was sticky with sweat by the time they walked back to the Community Center. A crowd had started to gather in the street. As they drew closer, he heard voices engaged in animated conversations. People were going in and out of the center and the glass door bounced reflected light across the street every time it opened.

"Curtis, good to see you. Looks like it's going to be a great turnout," said one man grasping Curtis' hand in a hearty handshake. It was Michael Sorenson, the grocery store manager.

"Yes, we're pleased with the number of people who came, Michael," said Curtis. "And I want to thank you for your donation. We appreciate it."

Curtis greeted a few others as he worked his way toward the front of the Center. Alicia stood behind one of the tables greeting people and handing out pamphlets and candles. She had re-gathered her hair on the top of her head, but he noticed tendrils of hair still escaped. She looked tired. Dark circles under her eyes marred her normally clear complexion.

He looked around at the crowd, the stage set with microphone and podium, and the chairs for the audience lined in perfect rows. Alicia had worked hard, he realized, and he felt guilty about their earlier argument. He walked over to where she stood behind the table.

"Appears we'll have a good crowd," he told her.

"Yes," she said and turned to talk with a man examining brochures.

"This is my daughter, Melody," Curtis said, after the man left.

"Hello, Melody," said Alicia. "I'm glad you could come."

"Alicia," said Curtis. He stopped, unsure what to say. "I want to apologize for this morning. You know." He shrugged. "You've done a fine job here and I, well, I wanted to say thank you."

Alicia had shifted from Melody to Curtis when he started speaking. She began to say something and then reconsidered. "Thank you," she finally said. She still looked tired and dark still encircled her eyes, but Curtis saw some of the tightness in her shoulders had eased. He felt suddenly awkward, unsure whether to step further into the uneasy truce between them. He noticed Mayor Pete Hamill try to catch his eye. The mayor stood next to the Police Chief McKinley and another man Curtis didn't recognize. Mayor Hamill waved Curtis over. Curtis nodded, held up a finger to indicate he would be there in a minute.

"Melody, I need to talk to the mayor before we start. Want to walk over with me?"

Just then a couple walked up to the table. With them was a boy about Melody's age.

"Oh, hi, Melody," the boy said. He had dark hair and eyes, and when he smiled Curtis saw white teeth against his brown skin.

"Hey, Justin," said Melody. "What are you doing here?"

Curtis looked at his daughter and then at the mayor's little group.

"Alicia?" he started to say.

She must have understood the question in his voice. She waved her hand as if shooing Curtis away.

"She'll be fine here. In fact, she can sit with me while you do the presentation."

Curtis put a hand on Melody's shoulder. "I'll be back in a minute, kiddo," he said, and went to join the mayor.

20

Rochelle

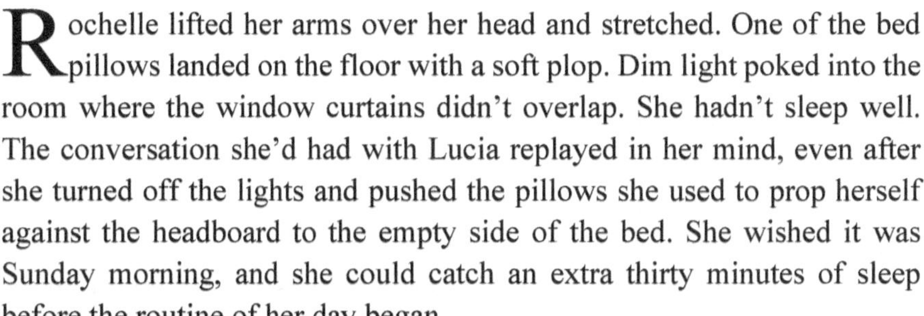

Rochelle lifted her arms over her head and stretched. One of the bed pillows landed on the floor with a soft plop. Dim light poked into the room where the window curtains didn't overlap. She hadn't sleep well. The conversation she'd had with Lucia replayed in her mind, even after she turned off the lights and pushed the pillows she used to prop herself against the headboard to the empty side of the bed. She wished it was Sunday morning, and she could catch an extra thirty minutes of sleep before the routine of her day began.

She had tried throughout the day yesterday to reach Lucia. At half past eight, when the sun was slipping below the horizon, Lucia finally answered.

"What do you want?" asked Lucia, after Rochelle identified herself.

Rochelle rehearsed this conversation in her head during the numerous times she had called Lucia's number only to listen to the phone ring into dead air. But when Lucia answered, all the carefully crafted sentences meant to smooth entrance into Lucia's grief vanished and her words arrived sounding sparse.

"I just wanted to see how you're doing," said Rochelle. "We ended on bad terms the last time we talked."

Silence hung on the line. Rochelle suspected Lucia hung up, except that she could hear breathing. She held her breath, trying to determine if it was her breath she heard, or Lucia's.

At last, Lucia spoke, "I'm doing fine,"

Her voice landed hard on the last word—turning the declaration she was fine to mean all was not fine and would never again be fine.

Rochelle asked if Lucia knew about the plans for the vigil. Yes, Lucia said, not that anyone had contacted her, invited her to the vigil, asked her to speak of her daughter. Rochelle questioned the failure to invite to a vigil the one most emotionally wounded by Marcela's death.

She knew the answer. Lucia's pain was like that of a wounded cat lashing out with teeth and claws. But still, the participants needed an icon, even an angry one, to remind them why they came together—the death of this mother's child, the result of bigotry and callousness. The organizers were afraid the mother's words would inflame instead of soothe, like the neighborhood needed. The organizers of the vigil realized that. Rochelle knew, too, and it worried her. She needed to gauge Lucia's anger so they could find a way to pay homage to the victim without the grieving mother invoking disaster.

"Lucia, I understand what you're saying, but lashing out won't bring your daughter back. It just makes it harder to heal. That I know. Please believe me."

"Of course, it won't bring my baby back. You think I'm stupid? But someone has to pay for killing Marcela."

"They will," Rochelle said, but knew Lucia wasn't interested in the court's methodical plod toward justice. Her anguish sought out the kind of hot justice that went back to the Old Testament, further back, even, when a tangible toll was assessed for a wrongdoing—an eye, or a hand, or the blood of a first child. That kind of justice was delivered hot, before contemplation and time cooled resentment.

"You know nothing of my pain." Those were Lucia's final words before she slammed the phone back into its receiver. Rochelle knew, as she had the first time, that Lucia's message was meant as a talon to rip the façade that Rochelle had so carefully crafted. When she heard the click of disconnect, Rochelle had gently placed the phone in its cradle, then shoved it onto the floor. It banged against the wall and sprawled across the rug. Only when AT&T's automated operator commanded her to check her phones because a receiver was off the hook, did Rochelle finally join the handset with the cradle and place the phone back on the side table.

The phone rang hours later, but Rochelle didn't answer it. Instead, she shook out the estrogen and other pills she took every day to maintain the veneer of herself and lined them up on the kitchen counter. She filled a glass from the kitchen faucet and, facing the kitchenette's dark window, swallowed the pills, one by one.

By the time Rochelle showered, dressed, and applied her makeup, she could hear sounds of activity in the street. She had decided to keep the shop open until after lunch. She hoped some of the traffic would find its way across the street and into her shop. It was late summer, and she still needed to clear out the inventory to make way for the Alpaca sweaters and wool ponchos she ordered earlier in the year.

Rochelle was rearranging the summer merchandise to make it more prominent when she heard the shop bell ring. She turned and was surprised to see one of the nuns from the *Casa de la Gente.*

"Good morning," Rochelle said.

"It's a great morning, actually. I'm Sister Clarice, by the way."

The nun held out a hand and smiled at Rochelle. The sun-worn skin around her eyes folded in on themselves until all Rochelle could see were bright pupils. Sister Clarice's eyes roamed the store and landed on the oak drawers stacked against the wall.

"Interesting," she said, fingering the cross that dangled on a chain around her neck.

Rochelle wondered what she was thinking. It was hard to read the little nun with her stern carriage and friendly eyes. Rochelle followed the nun's focus as she studied the cabinet.

"I heard some of our guests at *La Casa* talk about your shop," she finally said, turning to face Rochelle.

"Yes," said Rochelle, unsure where the conversation was going. She couldn't tell from the nun's demeanor if she disapproved or approved of the residents' visits. She waited for her to continue.

"Tell me a little about the substances you sell." Sister Clarice waved a hand at the bank of drawers.

Was the nun curious, or was there a motive behind her curiosity? *Abuela* Angelina was Catholic, had gone to mass every Sunday, but Rochelle, bruised by the Catholic dogma that God had not been wrong in gendering her as male, eventually refused to go. Some people, she knew, called what she sold voodoo medicine. Could be some of it was. The things Uncle Martin hid behind the curtain at the back of his shop could be viewed as pagan. She needed time to think. Rochelle pulled open a drawer. She pinched a few dried herbs and placed them in the palm of her other hand. She held the palm out to the nun.

"This is chamomile. When it's seeped in hot water it makes a tea that promotes sleep.

Sister Clarice nodded and pinched a little from Rochelle's palm. "Yes, I'm very familiar with chamomile tea. I fix myself a cup when I've had a worrisome day. Prayer and the tea," she smiled, wrinkles once again encasing her eyes, "allow me to sleep in peace."

"Did you know," Sister Clarice continued, "that prior to the Middle Ages, European monks preserved the knowledge of holistic medical care? In fact, monasteries often planted gardens of herbs and other plants that were used to treat common illnesses among the villagers."

"I knew the knowledge went back to primitive humans, but I didn't know the church was involved."

"Yes, yes. Of course, maintaining the knowledge fell out of favor at the end of the Middle Ages when people, usually the womenfolk using plants and such in holistic treatments, were accused of witchcraft. Well, enough of ancient church history. Tell me more about what you have."

Rochelle went to another drawer and pulled out a tied bundle of dried vegetation. "This is feverfew. It can be used in several ways. Seeped in water, it's a remedy for headaches, like migraine headaches. Made into a tincture, it's used externally to take the sting or itch out of insect bites."

Rochelle showed the little nun a few more, all benign, and far from the man-shaped mandrake root soaked in potent liquor that had been kept in the back of her uncle's shop. She wasn't sure how the nun would have reacted to something like the Mandrake with its pagan superstition and hallucinogenic properties.

As if the nun could read Rochelle's reservation, she said, "I served at a mission in Guatemala for many years. There, especially in the rural areas where we lived, the practice of nontraditional medicine went back to Mayan civilization. Those old ways influence inhabitants' lives, even to this day. We've lost a lot of knowledge about the link between the mind and the physical body. Science can explain how chemicals react in our brains, but there's still a lot they can't explain. I watched the shamans work with the indigenous peoples in Central America. Now, they understand the power of belief." She smiled at Rochelle. "I guess I don't need to tell you about that."

Sister Clarice still held the piece of chamomile pinched between her thumb and forefinger. She rubbed her fingers together, releasing the scent, lifted it to her nose, and sniffed.

"It smells fresh," she said. "I'd like to buy a bit of the chamomile, a quarter of a cup or so."

Rochelle moved behind the counter, pulled a scoop from underneath, and opened the chamomile drawer. There was more to this nun then the emphasis on church work that Rochelle had expected. Again, as if intuiting Rochelle's thoughts, Sister Clarice said.

"Religion is like that too. I mean the connection between mind and body and the power of belief and prayer. And I don't just mean being a Catholic. God, and the belief in one's god, is broader than just what is spoken in the Pope's chambers. Do you attend church?"

The nun's shift, from the wide topic of religion to the personal question, startled Rochelle. She stopped, looked at the old nun.

"Not much anymore, although, when I was younger, I went to mass with my grandmother. Then I moved to Miami for a while. Then Angelina, my grandmother, died." She folded the wax paper and poured the chamomile into a plastic bag.

"I see," the nun said. "But it is important to always be ready to greet God, because one never knows when we'll be summoned to appear before him."

"I understand," said Rochelle. She handed the bag to the nun. Sister Clarice paid for the tea, gave Rochelle one last crinkled smile and was gone.

The bell over the door chimed when the sister left. This time, the chime echoing through the store was eerily familiar to the bong of steeple bells calling parishioners. Rochelle shook her head. The little nun reminded her of Uncle Martin, the way both of them could talk in a tightening spiral around someone until they reached the nugget that contained the true character of that person.

The rest of the morning was busy. Rochelle only had five summer shirts left by midafternoon, when the last customer left the shop. She was pleased. There were still enough warm days ahead in September and she thought she could sell the rest of her summer stock. Rochelle turned the shop sign around to show it was closed and then stepped outside to noise and activity.

21

Curtis

————◇————

Curtis shepherded the four panel members up the stairs and onto the stage. First, was Kingston's mayor, Pete Hamill, then Police Chief Tom McKinley, and Parks and Recreation Director Marsha Gunderson. Sheriff Gerald Folsom was last. His breathing was labored as he climbed the steps and sat heavily on the folding chair. The chair gave an ominous creak, and Curtis recalled Amy's comment about Sheriff Folsom waddling after a crook.

He had met Marsha Gunderson a few days earlier. She told him she was a retired Army Sergeant. She was tall and muscled, with cropped grey hair. Curtis could easily envision her commanding the troops, whistle in hand. It wasn't a big leap from soldiers to commanding young ball players and the parks and recreation staff.

Doug Nguyen, Susie's husband appeared from behind the stage. He had volunteered to set up the sound system, as well as construct the water misting system to cool the audience.

"You're set to go," Doug said. His hands and face were dusty and streaked with sweat. Around his waist was a wide leather belt that sagged with the weight of his tools.

Curtis forced a deep breath and climbed the stairs to the stage. He tapped the microphone clipped to the podium and heard the magnified sound of his fingers. The crowd gathered in the street quieted.

"Good evening," Curtis began. "I'm happy to see so many people in attendance this evening and," he motioned to the other speakers sitting in folding chairs on the stage, "the representatives of our fine city." There was a smattering of applause and Curtis paused to let the sound die. "I'm glad to see such a great show of support, but the purpose of our gathering is sad. It is sad that it took the death of an innocent child, Marcela, to unite us against violence. It is a violence that arises from intolerance and from ignorance about others who are different."

Curtis had thought hard about the harshness of the word ignorance. He sat at the wobbly kitchen table the night before and wrote the speech. He had crossed out ignorance and replaced it with uneducated and then with uninformed, but those words turned the importance of what he wished to say to bland mush. In the end, he had kept his initial choice.

"Ignorance," he continued, "does not mean we are conceited, but only that we have not learned the value of cultures different from ours. We are not all that different—we all appreciate community, family and friends, and the celebration of important events."

He said a few more words but kept the speech short. Brevity made the message powerful, he had read somewhere. Curtis finished by thanking all those who helped. He looked at Alicia when he said it, but when he noticed Rochelle had joined Alicia and Melody, he pointed them out rather than just nodding his recognition.

He introduced Mayor Pete Hamill and listened as the mayor talked about the city's proposal to add multi-lingual staff to the police and sheriff departments and signage in three languages in the city offices. He only half-listened when Hamill segued into what he planned to accomplish if elected to another term.

"We've made progress to remake our city into a better place, but we still have a ways to go and I appreciate your support in our leading our community to a better place," Mayor Hamill said, as he ended his speech.

Marsha Gunderson took the mayor's place. She tugged down the hem of her dark gray suit jacket. Then she grasped both sides of the speaker's podium and said in a booming voice that didn't need amplification, "As most of you know, I've served in a number of different countries across the globe. I always made it a point to explore the different communities where I was stationed. What I discovered is acceptance is easy for children and youth. That is, if not influenced by the narrow-minded adults in their lives," she paused to emphasis her point, "the young will reach out and make friends with other children, even children with different customs and color. I saw that in the children of troop members stationed in Europe as well as on the northern coast of Africa. The way they connect is through play, whether that be organized sports or on their own. That is why baseball, volleyball, and the other sports sponsored by the Parks and Recreation Department are so important. That's why," she paused again, "we need both the financial and volunteer support of this community."

Gunderson went on, describing the department's services and positions where volunteers were needed, but Curtis was still thinking over what she said about children's play. She had a point. He looked at Melody.

She was sitting quietly beside Alicia who was talking animatedly with Rochelle. Melody told Curtis about her classmates. She had mentioned a Darcy, Thomas, Carlos, Tran, Mary Ann, Chau Hai. He was proud of his daughter, proud that she chose to attend a vigil for a girl she had never met. He now regretted he hadn't taken the time to listen to Marcela.

Would things have turned out different if he did? Maybe. Maybe not. He'd believed the words he wrote last evening, and he had believed them this evening as he stood in front of his townsfolk and spoke. It was too late for Marcela, but it wasn't too late for him.

Police Chief McKinley was next. "As you heard on the news the last couple of days, we have made arrests in connection with Marcela's arrest. Those cases are working their way through the criminal court system, and I want to emphasize this," he paused and scanned the crowd, "these cases will be resolved through legal means. I also want to make it clear," he motioned Sheriff Folsom to stand beside him, "that we will not tolerate any street justice." Again, he scanned the crowd, as if he could read the attendees' intents.

"The sheriff and I, as well as the other participants here, will take questions for a few minutes." He glanced at Curtis. Curtis nodded.

"Chief McKinley, we heard you're investigating incidents involving conflicts between gangs. Can you comment on that?" The question was from a newspaper reporter sitting in one of the front rows. He waved a notebook and that, plus his strident voice while the rest of the audience gathered their thoughts, caught the chief's attention.

"Tony," the chief said in acknowledgement, "as you know, we are aware of the situation and, as I said before, we will not tolerate any attempts at revenge. Next question," he said, deftly moving away from any more of Tony's questions about gang activity.

Curtis watched as a few more questions were asked. Then one was asked of him.

"Mr. Meyerson," a dark-skinned man said, "your panel," he pointed to the stage, "looks like our city did before the packing plants arrived. I was here to see it. My parents came up years ago from Mexico to work in the sugar beet fields. Why is the rest of our community not represented on your stage? Isn't that what this is all about?"

Curtis looked at the mayor and the two law enforcement officers, buying time. The crowd was quiet, as if holding their breath and waiting for his answer.

"You make a good point," Curtis finally croaked. We did ask Mr. Duc, Colonel Duc, to come, but I understand," he looked to the chief for support, "he has family issues. And," he pointed to a man standing beside the stage, "a representative of LULAC, Jesse Lopez, is here."

Curtis had planned to include Jesse on stage with the others, but the stage—really, it was just a flat-bed trailer—was small, and the League of United Latin American Citizens representative had offered to wait with Catholic Fathers Frank and Tran, and the Buddhist monk from Wichita for their turn in the program.

Curtis continued, "He and our religious representatives," Curtis pointed at the second group standing by the stage steps, "will speak next, before we walk down to the park."

"Second class, again," grumbled the man in the crowd.

"The chief and sheriff," Curtis said, attempting to steer the crowd in a different direction,"will respond if there any more questions."

He backed away from the podium. There was mumbling in the crowd, and people began to move restlessly. The feeling of accomplishment deflated, and he could feel the fractures as the community, once again, polarized into us and others.

The chief turned to Curtis, but by then Curtis had sat back down, wishing he had insisted Lopez sit on stage, wishing he had thought how the panel looked to the audience, wishing he could just disappear into his office.

"Let's switch now to the second panel in our program," the police chief announced. He motioned to the group beside the stage. There was a rumble of feet as the first panel left and the second climbed the stairs and settled in the vacated chairs.

Curtis stayed on stage. He listened as Jesse Lopez and the religious leaders spoke, spinning out the threads to stitch the audience together in a whole cloth. It was getting dark by the time the participants lighted their candles and started walking down the closed street to the park.

Curtis stayed behind to retrieve Melody.

"You did good, Dad," Melody said. He took her hand and squeezed it. She squeezed back. They trailed the crowd as they walked south through the darkening street. Candlelight flickered and danced across the building fronts. Curtis could smell the smoke and hot wax. One of the marchers began to sing. One-by-one, others picked up the melody. A little of the tension he felt when he had been on stage and the focus of attention, began to ease. It was hard to say what would remain of this evening's optimism as the weeks wore on. He was just grateful that his part in the celebration was finished, and he could relax and enjoy the rest of the evening.

He looked at his daughter and smiled. "I'm starving. What about you?"

22

Rochelle

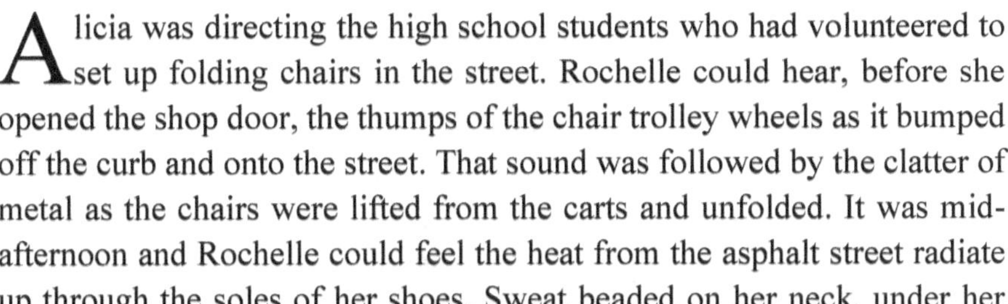

Alicia was directing the high school students who had volunteered to set up folding chairs in the street. Rochelle could hear, before she opened the shop door, the thumps of the chair trolley wheels as it bumped off the curb and onto the street. That sound was followed by the clatter of metal as the chairs were lifted from the carts and unfolded. It was mid-afternoon and Rochelle could feel the heat from the asphalt street radiate up through the soles of her shoes. Sweat beaded on her neck, under her hair. She twisted the hair, pulled a clip from her pocket and pinned the twist to the back of her head.

Someone had already set industrial fans in the shade on the other side of the street, but they had not yet been turned on. A man in overalls was constructing a framework of water misters above and between the big fans. As Rochelle watched, a pickup truck pulled a portable stage through the road barricades and stopped. The driver jumped out of the truck, wrenched down a support wheel from the tongue of the trailer, then disconnected the trailer and drove away.

"I'm glad you're here," said Alicia, when Rochelle walked over to her. "The kids have the tables set up already if you want to start spreading out the brochures and the candle stuff.

"Those need to go over here," Alicia continued, turning to direct two girls pulling another rack of folding stairs around the corner of the building.

"Molly," she said to someone else. "There's a cloth stage-apron inside in the lobby. Please get it and find someone to help you attach it to the stage." She pointed toward the trailer.

There was a loud crash. Rochelle turned and saw a cart of folding chairs had tipped when it went over the curb.

"Damn," said Alicia. "Be careful, girls," she said to the two teens now untangling the chairs that lay in a heap in the street.

"Sorry, Mrs. Rodriquez," one said, shrugging her shoulders.

"That's okay, Nancy. Just be careful. Please."

Rochelle fanned out brochures identifying the services provided by the *Casa de la Gente* and the Community Center along flyers listing the warning signs of domestic abuse and the the toll-free contact number. She stacked the cups she had slit the day before on another table but slid the boxes of candles under the table to shade them so they wouldn't soften in the sun. She was helping to carry out insulated containers of cold water and iced tea when she heard her name called. She looked up to see Curtis walking toward her. He was holding the hand of a girl with curly blond hair.

"Hi," Curtis said. "Glad to see you, again,"

His face was flushed. Rochelle wondered if he had gotten sunburned or if it was the heat that had prickled his skin.

"This is my daughter, Melody," he said.

The girl was older than Marcela had been, and without Marcela's delicate features. What Melody did have were the same intelligent eyes she had seen in Marcela. She saw interest flicker in them when the girl looked first at her dad, then at Rochelle.

"Hi," Melody said, giving Rochelle a little wave.

"Glad to meet you, Melody," Rochelle said. "Did you come to watch the vigil?"

"Yeah," replied Melody. Once again, she looked at her dad. There was an expectant look on his face. The girl shifted back to Rochelle. The three of them stood in awkward silence. Rochelle wished for a moment she was back in her shop, looking at the busy street through a pane of glass, like the screen on a television set.

"Well," Rochelle finally said, scrubbing a forearm with her hand. "Guess I'd better get back to work."

It was six-fifteen before the crowd found their seats and Curtis began introducing the panel members on the crowded stage. The big fans hummed as they blew air, cooled by misters, over the heads of the audience. Rochelle had counted the chairs—four sections, each with forty chairs. The chairs were all taken, and she estimated there was at least a fifty others standing or sitting on the curb. *A good turnout*, she thought as Curtis stood to talk. She scanned the audience looking for Jim. She couldn't see him, but there were other law enforcement officers from the police and sheriff's department roaming the edges of the crowd. They would pause and scan the audience, then move to a different place and do the same thing. Occasionally, they nodded or spoke with someone. She wondered if they were expecting trouble or just being cautious. Alicia sat behind one of the tables in front of the center away from the stage. She looked tired. Her face was drawn, and strands of hair had escaped from the ponytail at the back of her head. Beside her sat Curtis' daughter.

Rochelle made her way to the back of the audience and circled around to their table taking the empty chair beside Alicia. "You did a great job with everything," she said, when Alicia turned to her.

"Thank you," Alicia replied. She smiled wearily. "I'm just glad it's about over."

"Curtis giving you the day off tomorrow?" Rochelle asked.

"Right," Alicia said, drawing out the word as she rolled her eyes.

Melody cocked her head at the mention of her father's name, but didn't say anything.

Alicia and Rochelle turned their attention back to the panel of speakers when a man in the crowd rose. He said, "Your panel looks like our city did before the packing plants arrived. I was here to see it. My parents came up from Mexico to work in the sugar beet fields. Why is the rest of our community," he pointed to himself, and then at clusters of Hispanic and Vietnamese, "not represented on your panel?"

"Manuel Alvarez," whispered Alicia. "He has a point. White boys still run the city, and we're stuck doing the stoop labor."

Rochelle and Alicia continued to watch the exchange.

"And notice how no one really answers his question. They just talk around it," Alicia said, after Curtis cleverly punted the hot potato question to the police chief and sat down.

"Manuel's family owns the Buena Comida restaurant, right?" asked Rochelle.

"Yes, and he's on the board of the St. Guadalupe Catholic school. He's an asset to our community," she pointed at Rochelle and herself, "and he could be an asset to the city, but the great white founding fathers," she motioned to the stage, "can't recognize that."

Rochelle noticed that Melody had been listening carefully to their conversation. She worried the girl would report what Alicia said to her dad.

"Your dad is trying," she told Melody, wanting to protect Alicia from the consequences of her words.

The girl ignored her and turned back to watch her father thank the panel members. Rochelle wondered what Melody was thinking. She thought back to what Alicia had said, including Rochelle in the town's Hispanic society.

This time, she felt different about inclusion into the community of Mexican and Central Americans. It wasn't like when she was a child, similar in appearance to the other brown-skinned children, but with a different historical narrative from a Caribbean island. She leaned back in the chair, analyzed how it felt to belong somewhere. It was a connection that she hadn't experienced since she lived in Miami with its assortment of island immigrants—Cubans, Haitians, Puerto Ricans, Dominicans.

Movement on stage pulled Rochelle from her thoughts. She saw the police chief, sheriff, and mayor step off stage and four others step up. First, was Jesse Lopez, the local director of LULAC. Second, was the priest from Lucia's church. She recognized him as well as the Vietnamese priest from the other Catholic Church. She didn't recognize the last man climbing the stairs to the stage. He was a tall Vietnamese man with shorn hair, dressed in a saffron colored robe.

Curtis had remained on stage. He introduced the second panel. Jesse Lopez walked to the podium and Curtis sat down.

"Who's the guy in the robes?" whispered Rochelle.

"He's a Buddhist monk or priest—I'm not sure how they're titled— from Wichita," said Alicia. She leaned toward Rochelle. "I heard the nuns from *Casa de la Gente* let him hold services in one of their meeting rooms a couple times a month."

"Oh, I didn't know we had Vietnamese people practicing Buddhism here," said Rochelle. "I have customers who are Vietnamese, but I guess religion never came up."

"Yeah, I don't know much about it, either. Just what I heard."

Jesse talked first about knowing Marcela, then about the value of Hispanic culture to the whole community, how all must make the effort in order for the community to become better. He was good. Rochelle watched the audience smile when he recounted Marcela's pitch perfect music solo in the first-grade recital. She saw one cluster of audience members sit straighter when Jesse congratulated the high school LULAC club for painting fence railings and benches at the zoo's park. Jesse finished, the crowd applauded and then in unison the three priests rose and walked to the edge of the stage.

"Everyone please rise while my friends, the St. Guadalupe priest put one hand on the on the Vietnamese priest's arm and the other hand on the monk's arm, and I say a few words of benediction. There was a rumble of feet and chairs as people stood and bowed their heads.

Prayers were said in English, Spanish, and Vietnamese.

Then it was over. Rochelle watched people greeting each other. She had noticed when the crowd settled to listen to the panels that they were grouped together—Latinos with Latinos, whites with whites, and Vietnamese, by far the minority, with Vietnamese. Now, as people milled around, Rochelle noticed the lines demarking the different cultures lost their cohesiveness. The same thing had happened at the community meeting shortly after Marcela's death. It was good to see, although Rochelle wondered if tomorrow's dawn would again find people drifting back into the cloisters of their own culture, with its familiarity of language and custom.

"Everyone, please listen," said Curtis. He had remained on stage. He leaned forward, spoke into the microphone. "We need you to help stack the chairs back on their trolleys. Then, we'll make the walk down the street to the park. There will be food and drinks available, and we invite everyone to stay for a while."

The sky was darkening by the time the chairs were put away, candles were passed out and the crowd began marching to the park. One-by-one the candles were lit. Someone, she couldn't see who, lifted her candle, in its protective paper cup sleeve, above her head. The other marchers followed suit, lifting their candles high so the light flickered above the heads of the people and reflected in the storefront windows.

Rochelle followed the crowd and thought about the afternoon Marcela was shot. The gunshots and the sound of breaking glass had terrified her. She remembered crawling toward Valerie, cocooned in her own problems and unaware of the danger outside her own misery. She hadn't talked to Valerie since that terrible day. She'd call her tomorrow, see how she was doing.

"Amazing grace, how sweet the sound. That saved a wretch like me," a voice sang out. A hush fell over the crowd. Other voices joined the singer's, at first tentative, then strengthening until song filled the street. "I once was lost, but now am found, was blind but now I see." Rochelle felt goose bumps rise on her arms. She blinked to clear her vision that suddenly wavered like the light of candles.

23

Curtis

———◇———

I heard you had boys in custody for the shooting outside our community center, Chief McKinley," said Curtis. He and Melody had already gone through the food line. He piled slices of barbecued beef on slices of bread and added dill pickles and corn chips. Now, Melody was sitting on a park bench with a plate of food on her lap. Curtis perched beside her, one hand under the flimsy paper plate to keep it steady.

"Call me Tom," the Chief said. "Yes, we have a couple of juveniles and one eighteen year old in custody."

The chief picked a potato chip off his plate and popped it in his mouth, chewing with the same brisk efficiency that Curtis had observed in other law enforcement officers. He waited for Tom to go on and say more about the suspects in Marcela's murder. When he didn't, Curtis prompted him. "So, the case has been solved? The boys are going to be prosecuted?"

"They've had their first court appearances. A public defender will be assigned, likely for all three. Then, Judge Hamilton will determine whether the younger boy should be prosecuted as a juvenile or adult. He should have a decision soon on that matter. The cases, well, it takes time for them to work through the court system."

"Who are they? I heard one was old Colonel Duc's grandson."

"Yeah," the chief said, munching on another chip. "Juveniles, we can't officially release their names, but, yeah, guess everyone's heard the news by now. It was Duc's grandson. He's the youngest of the three."

"And the older two?"

"They're all friends. They're Vietnamese boys too. The eighteen year old, he's supposedly," Chief McKinley gestured one-handed quote marks around supposedly, "a member of the Dragon Boyz gang, although the gang doesn't have much of a presence in Kingston. They're well known to law enforcement. Lots of trouble, those two. The colonel's grandson, well, not so much trouble. The old colonel tries to keep a tight rein on the boy. It's too bad. Hard working family."

"Umm," Curtis said. He kept his eyes on the crowd milling around, hoped the Chief would say more. "A good family?" Curtis said when Tom stayed silent.

The chief waggled his hand back and forth in a so-so motion.

"Probably was a good family back in Vietnam. I know the colonel came from upper-class stock. The colonel's aunt, so the story goes, married some well-connected Frenchman back when the French Union troops were fighting against the communist Viet Minh forces. You know how the Vietnamese are, you don't just marry a person, you marry the whole damn clan."

"Not like here."

"Nah, here you're supposed to marry and move on with your independent life. Nuclear family and all that. Hell, I'm not sure it's a better way."

"I agree," Curtis nodded. His parents had fled to Florida and milder winters after his dad retired and sold the family farm. Curtis hadn't been interested in farming, and neither had his brother. His parents sold the farm equipment at auction and then sold the land. Brother Randy graduated with a degree in geology. He went to work in Houston for a big oil company. Curtis was the only one who stayed in the town where he was raised. There were some cousins still around, but the families hadn't been close, and he rarely saw them.

He and Amy had created their own little family, but their nuclear unit exploded and tossed him out. Now, he and Melody were it with his family. Maybe the old way was better.

"The colonel's whole family is here?" Curtis asked.

"Nah. The colonel came over with his wife and their son and daughter. He fought with the allied forces in the south, so our government greased the rails for them to come to the U.S. They landed somewhere in the east and then migrated here where they found work. His wife's gone now, died several years ago. He doesn't talk much about his son, I heard he works someplace back East. The daughter, that's the delinquent's mom, she works out at the packing plant. I'm not acquainted with her." He turned and grinned at Curtis, "Guess that just means we haven't crossed paths yet."

"The war was like that," said Curtis. Not that he had been in the war. He was in high school and college in the 1960s when the Vietnam War ran hot. That, and a lucky number in the draft lottery, had kept him out of the war and out of the grasp of the military. He was grateful. Three of his high school buddies had gone over. One came back in a body bag, and the other left a leg in south Asia's green, fetid jungle. He'd lost track of the third friend, Bobby Schmidt. Curtis knew Bobby had come back, but moved away shortly after, and they lost touch.

"I heard rumors that Antonio and his gang are going after the guys who shot his sister," Curtis said. He worried about being in their crossfire walking to his car when he worked late. The lot emptied quickly after six in the evening. By the time Curtis set the alarm and locked the door, his vehicle was alone in the corner of the asphalt lot.

It wasn't too much of a worry in August, when the sun didn't set until nine. It would become a concern when summer moved into fall and winter, and time changed from daylight savings to standard time. Then, dark came before six p.m. That's when he worried who lurked in the shadows, outside the glow of the lot's mercury lights. If he became director. No, he stopped himself. When he became director, he'd put up a sign next to the staff door announcing the parking space belonged to Center's director. That way, he could park just a few, well-lighted steps from the door.

"We're watching the Dragon Boyz and Antonio too," Tom said. "I know everyone's running scared, but the city's safe for most of us, the ones who aren't involved in the violence or drug trade.

Of course, there's Antonio. He's a wild card. That boy is hard to peg. He's smart, no doubt about it. That, plus, we haven't seen evidence he uses much what he sells." The chief poked his temple with an index finger, as if to emphasize that not using the drugs was a smart business move. "Makes it harder to nail him, and it makes it harder to predict what he's gonna do."

"Folks claimed Kingston was a safe place to live. No one locked their houses and kids roamed without fear. Or at least they did until the drugs, and the violence, spilled into our neighborhoods." Curtis said. "Of course, the girl was an innocent. She was just in the way when they went after Antonio. Hell, the same thing could happen to any of us." He tilted his head toward Melody. "Or our families."

Curtis worried about getting in the middle of a gang battle, but that wasn't the only thing that kept him away from the shadows when he walked to his car. After the shooting, the big cop with the strange tattoo, Sergeant Nicholas, told him Antonio was listening to something his sister was saying when the shooting started. What had Antonio been so intent on hearing that kept him from noticing the enemy swaggering down the other side of the street? Would Antonio come after him, blame Curtis's harsh words to Marcela for his lapse of attention?

That was the fear that woke him at two in the morning when a loud car drove past his apartment building. It caused him to check twice every night to make sure the door was double locked, and the windows were shut and latched.

"I wouldn't worry," said the chief, as if he read Curtis' thoughts. "We confiscated the guns they used, and we've gotten a couple of search warrants looking for other weapons. That's the real problem—guns in the wrong hands. In my day, yours too, we settled disagreements with fist-a-cuffs. No one was seriously hurt, and the loser slunk away. Now, they boost their egos with fire power. There's no honest battle in that."

Tom's focus shifted, and he stared over Curtis' shoulder.

"Chief?" Curtis heard someone say.

Curtis turned to find a young, uniformed officer.

"Excuse me," said Tom. He joined the officer and they walked to the edge of the crowd. Curtis watched the patrolman talk to Tom in a low voice. Occasionally, the chief nodded and lifted his head to look at the clusters of people gathered in the park.

Melody was talking animatedly with a girl about her age. A school friend, Curtis supposed. He picked up her plate, stacked it on his, and tossed them into a nearby trash barrel.

There must still be close to a hundred people milling around the food tables or talking with other participants. Curtis smiled and nodded to a couple walking past. They looked familiar, and he tried to recall their names. He spotted a tall woman with dark hair leaning against a picnic table, but it wasn't Rochelle. Then Curtis spotted Rochelle at one of the food tables. She was standing beside Alicia, spooning food out of a vat. She looked up and smiled, but the smile was aimed at the man standing in front of her holding a plate.

Melody had wanted a barbecued beef. He wished he'd known Rochelle was serving at the other table. If he did, he would have guided Melody toward her table. Now it was too late or, maybe not. Melody was occupied talking with her friend, and the line in front of Rochelle's table was short. He'd slip away for a few minutes, pick up a clean plate, and go through her line.

"Dad," Melody said tugging at his shirt. "Can Jennifer and I get some ice cream? It's homemade." She rubbed her tummy.

"Sure, honey, that sounds good," Curtis said. "I'll go with you." He could get a scoop of ice cream, then stop and talk to Rochelle. To Melody, he said, "I wouldn't want to lose you in the crowd." He put a hand on Melody's head, "You being so short and all, I can't see you."

Melody straightened and put her hands on hips, elbows jutting. "Dad, I've grown two inches since my birthday. I'm not a baby, anymore." This last was delivered with an eyeroll.

"No way." Of course, he could see Melody had grown, and it made Curtis sad to realize her cheeks were losing their little-girl plumpness, and her legs and arms were stretching. Soon, she'd be a teenager with friends and interests that didn't include him. It felt like another door closing on the life he had known before.

"All right," he told her. "But I'm still going with you. Ice cream sounds good to me too."

The ice cream was good. Even better, Rochelle greeted him as he walked past her table.

Curtis asked for the lemon custard with strawberries spooned on top. Melody chose strawberry and her friend picked vanilla that she topped with thick chocolate syrup. The ice cream was scooped from aluminum cylinders embedded in a trough of ice and plunked into plastic cups. He couldn't remember the last time he ate homemade ice cream. Amy never made it. "Why should I go to the work of making it when the store has so many flavors," she had explained when Curtis asked.

"Yummy," said Curtis, but Melody and Jennifer were concentrating on their own cups and didn't respond. He waved away a fly that wanted to share the cold desert and scanned the crowd. It had started to thin. People ate and left to tuck children into bed or to turn on television sets for the evening shows.

As he ate, Curtis watched Alicia and Rochelle. The line waiting for food was gone, and they were cleaning the top of the table. Alicia looked tired and tense. The dark circles under her eyes seemed even darker and she kept smoothing back hair that escaped her ponytail. She had done a lot of work to make the event successful. Maybe, he had been too hard on her. Tomorrow, he'd thank her; buy her a pot of flowers. It wouldn't hurt. One never knew what input Alicia might have in the selection process. If he became director. No, he was doing it, again. When he became director, he'd replace her with someone who didn't have allegiance to Dr. Kline, but it didn't have to happen immediately. Until then, he'd be kind. Plus, it looked like Alicia and Rochelle were friends. That could be useful too.

24

Rochelle

Rochelle stood behind one of the folding tables and spooned potato salad from a stainless-steel vat onto paper plates as people passed through the line. She scooped the last of the potato salad from the pan, and stood aside as a worker replaced the empty vat with one heaped with potato salad smelling of mustard and onion.

"Alicia," Rochelle said, after stout man asked for a second spoonful, "how much of this stuff do we have left? Think we'll run out?"

"I don't know," said Alicia. Guess we'll just going until it's gone." She lowered her voice and said in a stage whisper, "If you want some, better set a little aside."

Rochelle looked at the potato mixture. She had on thin latex gloves, but spooning from deep in the bottom of the vat had spread the mayonnaise and mustard mixture above the gloves and onto her arm. Between the tangy smell and the hot afternoon, she had lost her appetite.

"No, I'm fine. After this, I won't be able to stomach potato salad for weeks."

Alicia laughed. "I know what you mean."

"Smoked turkey, ham, or beef?" Alicia asked the woman standing in front of her, plate in hand.

"Turkey," said the woman and Alicia used tongs to lift thin slices of meat onto the woman's sandwich bread.

Rochelle added a scoop of the potato salad to the plate, and the line moved forward. Finally, the parade slowed. Rochelle saw the crowd had thinned, but there were still people standing around talking, or sitting in groups at the picnic tables. Others stood in line waiting their turn for ice cream. Rochelle took a damp towel from behind the potato salad and wiped dribbles of food from the top of the table.

"Mrs. Kline," said Alicia, "I'm happy to see you again."

In front of Alicia was a thin, older woman with stiff blond hair. Behind her, holding her elbow, stood a man who appeared to be in his late forties. The man had the same wide cheekbones and aquiline nose the woman exhibited. His hair was shot through with silver. Handsome.

Rochelle shot him her most alluring smile.

"Good to see you again, Alicia. This is my son, Alex."

There was an awkward pause as Alex extended his hand to Alicia and Alicia held up gloved hands.

"And this," Alicia said motioning with tongs, "is Rochelle Sanchez. She owns the shop across the street from the community center."

"Nice to meet you," said Emily Kline.

"Same here," said Alex. My dad told me about your shop with all the homeopathic treatments. I find it interesting."

He looked attentively at her, and Rochelle felt warmth spread through her chest.

"Alex is a medical doctor," Emily said. "He works at a hospital in Connecticut."

"Are you back for a visit?" asked Alicia.

"Well, yes and no," his mother said. Her voice faltered.

Only then did Alex break eye contact with Rochelle and move beside his mother. He put an arm around her shoulder, and she pressed into his side.

"Dad's in the hospital again," Alex said. "It's more serious this time, so I came back."

"Alex is very busy with his practice," said Mrs. Kline. "I told him we would be fine—he didn't need to make the trip."

She pulled a tissue from her purse and wiped her eyes.

Alex looked at Rochelle and Alicia over the top of his mother's head. From his grim expression, Rochelle suspected Dr. Kline wouldn't be going home this time.

"We're very sorry to hear that," said Rochelle.

Alicia seemed stunned.

Emily folded the tissue back into her purse. She was still tucked under Alex's arm, as if gathering strength from her son. "My husband was pleased to hear about the vigil. We arrived late, but I wanted to see how it went so I can tell Mark. He'll be happy to know the community has been supportive."

"Tell Dr. Kline we wish him well," said Rochelle. She waited a moment for Alicia to say something, but Alicia remained silent, trying to digest the news.

Mother and son moved on down the food line. Beside her, Alicia mechanically asked, "turkey, beef, or ham," and forked sliced meat onto plates. Occasionally, Rochelle heard Alicia sniff, but didn't say anything, wanting to give her time.

Finally, Alicia spoke in a hoarse voice, "I always believed Dr. Kline would get better and everything would go back to normal."

Rochelle shook her head. "I suspect it won't happen this time." She felt the same dread talking with the Klines that she had experienced when Angelina's doctor told her it was time to summon the family. The doctors knew, and Rochelle had recognized, that her *abuela* was failing. It was time to assemble the family to say a last goodbye and witness the transition from life to whatever afterlife there was after the last breath escaped one's body.

At last, the line of people waiting to fill their plates thinned, then shifted to another table where ice cream was being served.

"Let's put this stuff away, shall we?" said Alicia.

"Good idea." Rochelle understood her need to stay busy so Alicia didn't have time to contemplate both Mark Kline's shortened future and her own, now that Dr. Kline would not be returning to dislodge Curtis.

Rochelle was carrying a half-empty pot of potato salad to the refrigerated grocery truck when a lady walked up to her.

"Here, I'll take that," the woman said. "The man over there," she nodded her head toward the front of the truck, "said he wants to talk with you."

Rochelle looked but didn't see anyone.

"Who?" she asked, not ready to hand off her kitchen duties for someone she didn't see.

"That man over there," the woman pointed toward the truck. "The big blond guy. Good looking. Muscles." The woman pantomimed broad shoulders. "I think he's with the police. I've seen him before."

"Oh," said Rochelle. She handed the pot she was carrying to the woman and pulled off the latex gloves. "Thanks, I know him."

Rochelle felt guilty leaving. Cleaning up, she had entertained a daydream of Alex Kline. She envisioned him, the handsome doctor of every lusty woman's dream, in her apartment. They would eat an intimate dinner by candlelight, no potato salad at this dream dinner. Then Rochelle would turn on her favorite romantic music—something slow and bluesy by the *Motown Spinners*—and they would mesh their bodies, and dance slowly around the room. Dr. Alex would run his hands over her breasts, down her waist, and then begin to slide the skirt up over her hips.

That's where the daydream ended like all the other ones—with a sound like a needle screeching across a vinyl record—right before the lifted skirt revealed what hid under it.

"Jim," Rochelle whispered as she rounded the truck to the dark backside. "Where are you?" A figure in dark jeans and a black tee stepped away from the dark shadow cast by the truck. "Oh," Rochelle said, jumping at his unexpected closeness. "You scared the hell out of me. I didn't see you in the dark."

"Hey, baby," Jim said.

"You're not working tonight?" was the only thing she could think to say.

"I'm working. Just not wearing the uniform tonight. Makes it easier to blend in with the crowd."

"Blend in, are you serious, Jim? Everyone—the bad and the good guys—recognizes who you are."

"Yeah, I know," Jim said. He looked her over and took her arm by the wrist, pulled it toward him and licked. "Yummy, you taste like potato salad and I'm hungry."

"What imagination," she said, pulling away and laughing. "I washed it all off."

"You still smell yummy." He leaned in to sniff her hair. "*Odeur* of mayonnaise and mustard with just a hint of sweet pickle relish."

Rochelle wanted to scoop up the leftover potato salad, smear it down her throat and over her chest—enjoy it as Jim licked it off. What she said was, "So, you're here watching the crowd? Are you expecting problems?"

"Haven't seen any, yet."

"I didn't see you at the vigil," she said.

"I was around. I saw you." Jim glanced around, made sure no one was watching, and kissed her.

Rochelle smelled Jim's aftershave, felt his lips, then his tongue as it flicked along the inner edge of her lip. Crowd sounds faded. They were in another place now, apart from the noise and bustle on the other side of the truck. A clanging noise, like a pot being dropped, jerking Rochelle back from their private retreat. She pulled away.

"Damn," said Jim. "Later?"

"Yes," said Rochelle, her breath coming quick.

They held each other, neither ready to part.

Rochelle said, "So, everything quiet then? No problems?"

"Calm so far. Antonio is here with his mom. Saw them arrive a few minutes ago."

"Lucia's here? Now, I'm worried. I've talked to her a couple of times since Marcela died."

"And?"

"She's angry, vengeful is more like it. The anger, I can understand it. That's normal after losing a child under those circumstances. The revenge, that's something different. That kind of thing is harmful, gets in the way."

"She wants revenge against the boys who shot Marcela? Can't say that's unexpected."

"Sure, against the boys. But it goes deeper than that."

Nicholas shrugged. "Well, the lady has been pissed off for a long time. At the world and everyone in it, from what I hear. Now, she's left with the one kid that causes her the most angst."

Jim pulled away from Rochelle, shifted to cop attitude. "Not the happy family she envisioned, I imagine."

"That's true. The organizers—including Curtis—didn't invite her to the vigil, did you know that?" Rochelle said. "Of course, they didn't mail out invitations, but I think someone should have called her, extended a personal invite."

Jim grinned. "She's like a pissed off porcupine. I'd guess no one wanted to get in range of her quills."

Rochelle smiled at the image.

"You're right," she said. She ran a hand along Jim's muscular forearm. "Lucia always has been bristly. Do you think she or Antonio will start anything tonight?"

"We have eyes on them. Plus, we confiscated their guns when we searched both Antonio's and the Vietnamese boys' houses."

"It's not like they can't find other weapons."

Jim cupped Rochelle's chin in his hand, said, "You know I'll protect you."

Rochelle had a sudden memory of her mother squatting in front of her, holding her chin in just this same way and telling her, "*Niño*, I will always protect you." Later, her mom would only stand by and wring her hands as a boyfriend, one in a string of many, beat Rochelle with a Concho studded belt, shouting, "I'm gonna beat the fucking fairy out of you, boy."

She pulled her chin out of Jim's hand. "I can take care of myself."

The words landed harsher than Rochelle intended. Jim took a step back, started to say something. Before she could his radio crackled. Rochelle heard a voice,

"Sergeant Nicholas. Jim. Where are you?"

Jim unclipped the radio from his belt and spoke into it. "I'm at the west edge, checking around the backside of the supply trucks."

Jim looked a Rochelle and mouthed, "Later." He squeezed her shoulder, turned, and strode back toward the park.

"We need eyes on," she heard the voice on the police radio say, but the rest of the transmission was lost when Jim rounded the front of the truck.

25

Curtis

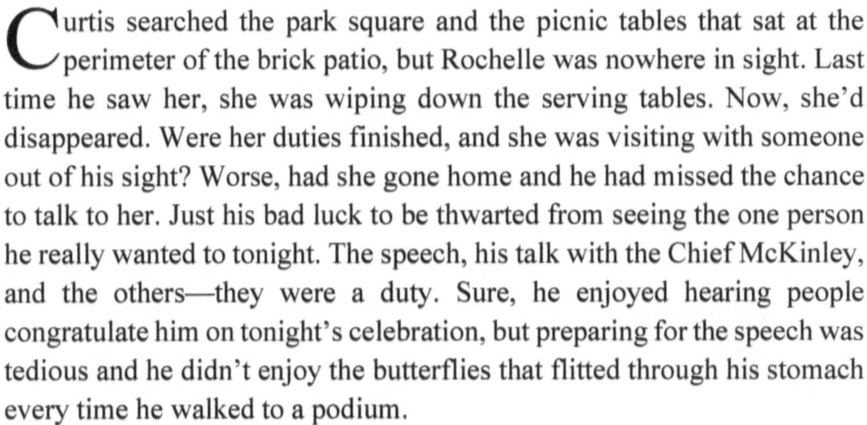

Curtis searched the park square and the picnic tables that sat at the perimeter of the brick patio, but Rochelle was nowhere in sight. Last time he saw her, she was wiping down the serving tables. Now, she'd disappeared. Were her duties finished, and she was visiting with someone out of his sight? Worse, had she gone home and he had missed the chance to talk to her. Just his bad luck to be thwarted from seeing the one person he really wanted to tonight. The speech, his talk with the Chief McKinley, and the others—they were a duty. Sure, he enjoyed hearing people congratulate him on tonight's celebration, but preparing for the speech was tedious and he didn't enjoy the butterflies that flitted through his stomach every time he walked to a podium.

There was his daughter, Melody. He loved the girl, enjoyed spending time with her, more so since he had been relegated to part-time father. But still, didn't fatherhood fall more on the responsibility side of the equation than the pleasurable side, where he was free to pursue his own interests— like flirting with Rochelle.

"Hey, sweetie," he said to Melody. "Are you done?" She had finished her ice cream and was wiping her hands on the soggy napkin. "You gonna be okay for a minute here with your friend while I look for something to clean our hands with?"

"Sure, Dad," Melody said, and turned back to her friend.

A few people still stood in line, bowls in hand, for the last of the ice cream. Near them was a rack that held rolls of paper tools. The park's water fountain was located beside the towel rack. Curtis pulled off several sheets of paper towels. He took a long drink of water, then wet the paper towels and wrung out the excess. Folding the wet towels, he added extra dry sheets.

He was on his way back to Melody and her friend when he saw Rochelle emerge from behind one of the trucks. Curtis took a quick look around to make sure no one was making their way toward him, then made his way toward her, selecting a path through the thinning crowd that would intersect with her.

"Hey there, Rochelle," Curtis said, when they drew close. He tried to act nonchalant, like meeting her had been an accident rather than deliberate. His hands were still damp from holding the wet towels. He wiped them as best he could on the dry ones.

Rochelle turned to Curtis. She was so beautiful. Even after being out in the heat all afternoon, she still looked cool and composed. She had on a yellow and orange sundress, pinched in at the waist in a way that emphasized the curves of breasts and hips. Her long hair was pulled back into a knot that, unlike Alicia's, had remained silky and smooth in the heat. Large gold hoop earrings completed the picture.

Curtis lost the line of conversation he had so carefully composed in his head. All he could think to say was, "Seems we had a good turnout."

Rochelle smiled. "Yes, it was a good thing to do, this vigil."

It was a beautiful smile, one that lit her face. A warm feeling spread through Curtis. She was pleased with what he had done. Should he ask her what she thought of his speech? Would that make him appear vain? He considered, said, "It's been hard work, but I think it will pay off, bring people together. The Center might sponsor other community events." Planning other events would give him a chance to spend time with Rochelle. Curtis loved the sound of her name, how the tongue curled to form the "R" sound then pushed past the lips in lush sound. He watched her breathe, the rise and fall of those high breasts. He leaned forward and tried to catch her scent.

"Yes, it was a good idea Alicia had," Rochelle said. "You're lucky to have her working for the Center."

Curtis pulled back, looked at her.

"Alicia?" he asked, confused. He felt disorientated, like the conversation had turned a corner he didn't expect.

"Yes, Alicia reached out to the community leaders, even asked me to help."

"I worked hard too." Curtis heard his tone, like that of child who had been caught copying a classmate's homework, but it was out of his mouth before he could stop it.

Curtis felt her eyes assessing him, calculating his measure. She nodded, "Yes, Curtis, you contributed in your way too."

Curtis couldn't tell if her remark was patronizing or sincere. It was hard to read this woman. If they could spend more time together, he would be able to figure her out.

He realized he still held the damp paper towels. He looked for Melody, remembering he had left her sitting next to her school friend. He saw only her head, a head with curly, blond hair pulled back from her forehead with a silky headband. She was focused on something. Curtis followed her gaze and saw Alicia standing behind one of the serving tables with several other people. One was a girl a little older than Melody with dark, wavy hair. It was Alicia's daughter. He recognized her from visits at the center. A younger boy stood next to Alicia. Curtis guessed the boy was her son. The other person was the thin, stoop-shouldered lady he had seen earlier with her baggy clothes and gaunt face. Alicia was motioning Melody to come to them.

When Curtis turned back to Rochelle, he found she was also watching the interaction between Alicia and Melody.

"My daughter," said Curtis, pointing to Melody.

"Yes, you introduced us earlier."

Damn, he had forgotten. "Her mother and I are divorced, now," he continued. "I normally get Melody on the weekends, but she wanted to come today. I think it's a good idea for her to watch her dad at work. Don't you?"

"Sure," said Rochelle, but Curtis saw she was no longer listening to him. Instead, she was focused on Alicia and the woman. Alicia bent toward Melody and said something. Then Alicia pointed to the older lady. She put her hand on the back of Melody's shoulder, as if prompting her. Melody stepped close to the older lady, put out her hand, and said something. Curtis couldn't hear what they said, but after a short time the lady accepted Melody's hand.

Curtis faced Rochelle, tried to draw her attention. "I'd like to come by sometime and check out the herbal remedies you have in your shop. I heard you have some fascinating things."

Rochelle, eyes still on Melody, Alicia, and other lady said, "That's fine. I'm open most days, nine to six or so."

She seemed distracted, and Curtis worried he was losing his chance with her. He tried to formulate the cautious words needed to ask Rochelle if she was married, even though he had already checked and found no ring on her left hand. If she wasn't married, did she already have a special someone in her life? She was young and pretty, there probably was someone. But she had come alone to the celebration. If she was serious about someone, wouldn't he have been here with her? The fact she came alone and spent her time working the food line gave him hope. He just needed to ask the question.

"I was wondering," he began.

"That's Lucia," Rochelle said, still watching.

"Lucia?" Curtis repeated. The name sounded familiar, but he couldn't place where he had heard it.

"Lucia, Marcela's mother," said Rochelle.

Now he remembered why the name was familiar, it was in Marcela's obituary.

"Why was no invitation extended to her?" asked Rochelle.

Her voice was soft, but her eyes had hardened. The dark irises, once inviting, were flinty.

"What? Well." He couldn't find the words, didn't know the answer. "It was a public event. We put up posters around the neighborhood. No one was specifically invited. It was supposed to be for anyone who wanted to come. Why would we send an invitation to her?" The last was delivered in a stronger voice.

"Lucia is Marcela's mother. The intention of this," Rochelle motioned at the supply trucks and cluster of people who remained, "was to memorize Marcela, put a spotlight on the violence that comes from seeing ourselves as only 'us and 'them.' Someone should have called her. I know she wouldn't have wanted to speak on stage. She's still angry. I understand that. Maybe, hers is not the voice we needed to hear tonight. But someone should have reached out to her."

"I, I," Curtis started to say, "I, Alicia, we." He was fumbling badly. Had Alicia not called the girl's mother? He remembered Rochelle raising the question in one of the planning meeting. He thought Alicia had, well he hadn't asked her, but he assumed she would have made the call. He tried to recall the meeting. The conference room was full. Was Alicia even present to hear Rochelle voice the question?

There was a noise behind him, and he saw Rochelle's attention shift. He turned and saw three young Hispanic men talking among themselves in low voices. Occasionally, they lifted their heads, and their eyes roamed the crowd as if looking for someone. One of the youths had a plump body. The bare arms protruding from his muscle shirt were fleshy with little muscle definition. The other two were slender, and the arms protruding from their shirts had ropy muscles, the kind that came from the repetitive movements of heavy work, rather than lifting gym weights. One of the thinner men had a shaved head, and a tattooed tear in the corner of his eye. He looked like a gangster. Curtis recognized the man in the middle—Antonio. Their appearance worried Curtis.

"Excuse me," Curtis heard Rochelle say. He turned to her, but she was watching the three youths. As she turned to leave, she put a hand on Curtis' arm. Her touch made his arm tingle, and he felt himself harden.

26

Rochelle

Rochelle waited a minute, then followed Jim's path around the front of the truck. She thought she had put all the bad memories of her childhood behind her until Jim had grabbed her chin and a fetid bubble of memory burst to the surface. She hadn't meant to lash, make him the target for something that had happened years ago, but she could take care of herself. She'd proven that during her years in Miami when exiting a gay bar was often an invitation to those who liked to taunt or bash the patrons. It had made her vigilant of her surroundings and the moods of people she passed in the streets. Rochelle had even taken classes in Taekwondo from old Korean man who ran a dojang down the street from Uncle Martin's shop.

As she walked through the stragglers who remained in the park, she saw Curtis head toward her. She shifted direction, angling away, but Curtis adjusted his path to intercept her. He'd been watching her. She was aware of it because whenever she scanned the crowd, she would find him watching. She'd talk to him a few minutes, try and deflect his curiosity, politely decline the invitation she saw so plain in his face.

"Evening, Curtis," Rochelle said, when their paths intersected.

"My daughter," Curtis said, and pointed to a curly headed girl talking to Alicia. It was clear he loved his daughter. That was as plain to Rochelle as the pain she saw on Curtis's face when he told her he was divorced. It was the despair she often saw on men's faces when they came into her shop looking for remedies for lagging libidos, or the secret tonic that would create strong bodies and sharp minds. They rarely admitted their desperate need for vindication to the wives and girlfriends in which they trusted their delicate hearts. Instead, they assigned their depression and loneliness to the failure of the organ that hung between their legs. If Curtis could convey the same care he exhibited as a father to the rest of his life, he would accomplish more. But today, he still had work to do.

"I'm curious," she said, interrupting his single-minded pursuit, pushing him in a different direction, "Why was no invitation extended to her?" Marcela's mother, Lucia, she meant. She had pointed Lucia out to

Curtis, but based on his reaction he didn't recognize who she was. He stumbled over the rational, the blame actually, for not inviting Lucia. Rochelle was only half listening to Curtis' clumsy words when something else captured her attention.

Antonio stood at the edge of the lingering crowd. On one side of him was Marcus, Antonio's friend since childhood. Marcus was a chubby child, and he had grown into a soft adult spending too much time on his mother's couch eating potato chips and watching television. Marcus was no threat but Choco, the hard-eyed one on Antonio's other side with his macho posturing, shaved head and tattoos, was a different story. The three, with Antonio in the center, had their heads together, talking in low voices. Occasionally, one of the three would pop his head up and look around if trying to spot someone. As she watched, Antonio lifted his head and saw his mother. A look passed between mother and son. Rochelle didn't know what message the look conveyed, but it worried her.

"Excuse me," she said to Curtis. She touched his arm when she walked away, a command for him to stay and not follow her. Where in the hell was Jim? She wondered if the police knew Antonio was here. Had his appearance prompted the radio voice that commanded Jim to put eyes on something? She'd walk to the three teens and talk to them, redirect their intention, whatever it was, until the officers arrived.

She took a couple steps forward before she saw Jim and two uniformed officers step behind the three youths. Antonio and his two companions turned in unison and froze when they saw who it was. The two uniformed officers stood back, legs apart, and watched. One of the officers rested a hand on the butt of his gun. Jim, even in jeans and T-shirt, was clearly still in charge. The situation looked tense, both the police and the three teens stood square against each another. No one moved, except Choco who flexed his hands into fists.

Jim stepped in front of Antonio. Rochelle couldn't hear what he was saying. Antonio's back was toward her so she couldn't read his expression, but after a minute he shrugged and raised his hands, palms open. Jim moved close, spun Antonio around, and pulled his hands behind his back. With his other hand, he patted Antonio down while the two uniformed officers guarded Antonio's friends. Antonio spotted Rochelle when Jim turned him. He smirked at her as Jim ran his hands down Antonio's torso and legs. When Jim ran his hand under the waistband of his jeans, Antonio shifted and thrust his crotch at Rochelle.

Antonio's smirk made Rochelle's skin crawl, but she stood her ground as Jim finished the search, pointed to the ground, and said something. Antonio sat. Jim moved on to Antonio's friends. Marcus looked flustered when Jim searched him. He tried to move away as the sergeant ran his hands down Marcus' sides and bulging belly. Jim must have tightened the grip on Marcus hands because he winced. He was trembling by the time the search was over. The last man, Choco, did not fidget when searched. He stood stiffly, giving no quarter to the indignity of the sergeant's touch. His face was tight, and his eyes bored into the distance, at something only he could see. Rochelle moved to one side to avoid the aim of those eyes.

The search was done efficiently and quietly. A couple of people watched, but soon went back to their conversations, as if the police presence allayed any fears.

Jim caught Rochelle's eye after the search was completed and Antonio and his friends moved back through the crowd, away from where she stood. He nodded once to her and then opened his hands to indicate they had found no weapons. Rochelle let out the breath she didn't know she had been holding. She looked at her watch. It was almost ten o'clock. She'd check with Alicia and make sure everything was done. A long bath to wash away the day's sweat and tension sounded good. Then she'd dim the lights, pour a glass a wine, and wait to see if Jim called.

27

Curtis

———◇———

Curtis wanted to clutch the hand Rochelle placed on his arm and tell her how much he enjoyed talking to her. He wanted, if he was honest about it, to savor the warmth of her skin, but now she was gone, and the moment had escaped.

He found her at the edge of the park's center patio. Her arms were folded tight across her chest as if she was trying to hold herself steady. She was watching three young, Hispanic men. Behind them were two uniformed police officers and a man he recognized in black jeans and T-shirt. It was the police sergeant, Jim Nicholas.

Curtis wanted to go to Rochelle, but there was something about the intense way she was staring at the group that stopped him. Sergeant Nicholas turned the man standing in the middle, so he faced Rochelle. He pulled the man's hands behind his back and used his other hand to search him.

The young man being searched had grown a goatee since he last saw him, but Curtis recognized who he was—Antonio, Marcela's brother. Sergeant Nicholas ran a hand down one side of Antonio's torso and then the other. Antonio's expression was stony, but when the sergeant ran his fingers under his waist band, he smirked. Jim looked at Antonio's face, saw the smirk, and pulled him sideways to finish the search.

If it was him, he would have searched the big guy with the shaved head first. He looked the most threatening with the tattooed mark, like an inked tear, below his eye. Curtis remembered reading an article about the significance of a tattooed tear. Something about earning it by killing someone, or maybe the tear memorialized someone who had been killed. He couldn't recall which now.

Curtis hadn't seen Antonio since that terrible afternoon when he was crouched on the pavement in a pool of his sister's blood. He looked different now, and it wasn't just the goatee. It was no wonder he hadn't recognized him at first. Any sorrow that had diminished Antonio's stature the day he held his dead sister's body was gone. Now he stood, lean and muscular, eyes defiant. Curtis watched as Sergeant Nicholas go through the same search of the other two men. What he didn't see were any weapons the trio had. That was good. They didn't need to deal with any more violence on this day that was supposed to represent a step toward peace.

A few people still lingered in the park. He was surprised to see Colonel Duc talking animatedly in Vietnamese to several couples. Curtis didn't know what they were saying but their posture looked relaxed. Often, they would nod and smile at something one of them said. One of the men in the group pointed at Curtis and said something to the colonel. The colonel saw Curtis and raised a hand in greeting. He spoke to his friends, gave a small bow, and went to join Curtis.

"A good turnout, yes?" Duc said after he greeted Curtis.

"Right. I'm—we're—happy with the numbers." Curtis paused for a minute, "And the diversity too. I should thank you for that. But it would have been better if you had been part of the panel of speakers."

"Not a wise idea," said the old colonel, a puzzled look on his face. "Did you not know that my grandson was arrested for his involvement in the little girl's," he cleared his throat, "death?"

"I heard, but they can't hold you responsible for something your grandson did, can they?

"I hold myself responsible. We, our family, all have responsibility."

Curtis didn't know what to say. A parent may be legally responsible for a child's actions, but was a grandparent? Plus, the boy wasn't a child. He was nearly an adult with his own will and responsibilities.

Suddenly, Curtis had an idea. He rocked on his feet, thinking it through. This might be the one idea he could truly claim as his own. It would be his piece in the effort to mend the damage the girl's death, and the clash of cultures and competition for jobs, had caused. Sure, he had spearheaded plans for the vigil, but in truth it was Alicia who initiated the plan. And the daycare scholarships? He presented the idea to the center's board, but it was the two nuns who had suggested it. But this. This was his idea. It would be the coup that he could carry with him into the job as the new director.

He turned to the colonel, "You're right. When a member of a family does something it reflects on the whole family. I know that's especially true in your culture."

Curtis saw he had the old man's attention. He continued. "The same is true in Hispanic families, you know, where the younger members are raised by the whole family—parents, aunts and uncles, grandparents." He pointed to his chest, "We, unfortunately, have lost some of that family continuity. We form nuclear families and a lot of us have moved away from our parents." A nuclear family was the way Curtis thought it should be with each unit of father, mother, children creating their own future instead of being locked into the mesh of extended family expectations, but it wouldn't bode well to mention that.

He paused giving Duc time to think about what he said and to formulate what he needed to say next. The old man was listening. He nodded as if in agreement.

Curtis continued. "What we need to do is get the older, more mature, generation involved in healing the community after what happened to the little girl."

He paused again. He'd snagged Duc's attention. Now it was time to reel him in. "Do you think that is right? The whole family needs to participate?"

The old man shrugged, looked down at his feet.

"The argument was between the girl's brother and your grandson's group." He thought group sounded better than gang, although weren't gangs the real problem in this situation?

"Marcela's mother is here tonight. I'd like to introduce you to her."

The old man shook his head. "I don't think it's a good idea."

"But you said the whole family is a unit?"

"Yes, of course," said Duc.

"We have to start somewhere," said Curtis. He stopped talking. He hoped Lucia was still around. She was.

Alicia had gathered her kids, and he watched the family walk toward their car. Rochelle was talking with Lucia, and Melody stood beside them. Marcela's mother looked as thin and worn as the old colonel in her baggy blouse and pants. A big purse, as worn as Lucia, was slung over one shoulder.

"I'll introduce you," Curtis said to Duc. "No one has to wave a white flag at this point. It's just a simple acknowledgement. You can say what you want, or just say nothing. Then, we'll shake hands and go our own ways."

The old man looked at Lucia. "Maybe, a good thing to say is—we are sorry for her loss."

"Yes," said Curtis. He had done it. It felt good. He touched Duc's arm and gently nudged him forward.

His daughter pointed at her wrist and then in the direction of their parked car. Curtis looked at his watch. It read 9:35. Curtis had promised Amy he'd bring Melody back by nine o'clock. He'd lost track of time. It would be okay, he'd introduce Duc to Lucia and then he'd drive Melody home. They'd be a little late, but he'd talk to Amy, tell her he was on track to become director and that came with certain responsibilities.

Melody came to meet him. She skipped the first couple of steps toward Curtis then slowed to a walk. Ever since she was toddler, Melody had done that hop, skip, walk routine when she was excited about something. It made Curtis happy to see she hadn't yet lost this bit of childhood exuberance. He looked past her to Rochelle and Lucia. This was perfect. Rochelle was there to witness him introducing Colonel Duc to Lucia. She would nod her approval and look at him with a new admiration.

As Curtis and the old colonel made their way toward them, Lucia turned her back to Rochelle. Rochelle shrugged a shoulder and turned to leave. Curtis took a couple of quick steps, trying to hurry Duc. Then Lucia caught sight of Curtis and Colonel Duc walking toward her. She frowned and there was something unsettling in her expression. Colonel Duc put a hand on Curtis's arm.

"Wait," he said.

Did the man now want to back out? He saw his plan begin to unravel. Curtis opened his mouth, preparing to ask the old man what the problem was, but Duc was watching Lucia. He tensed.

Curtis saw Lucia twisted the baggy purse around to her front and pull something out. It was a pistol, black and huge in Lucia's hand. She pointed it at them. She used both hands to hold the heavy weapon, but the barrel still shook. Beside him, the old man said something in Vietnamese. Curtis suddenly realized Melody was still walking toward him, unaware what was happening behind her.

"Oh, damn," Curtis hissed. He shouted and ran toward Melody. Melody froze, a look of surprise on her face. He took one last stride, grabbed his daughter, and twisted her behind him.

There was an explosion, then another. Momentum pulled Curtis and Melody to the ground, his body shielding hers. He heard Melody grunt an "olf" as they landed. Hot pain tore through his chest and blood pounded in his ears. He was aware of time passing, but time had become skewered, and he couldn't tell how much had passed. Melody wiggled underneath him.

"Dad," she said. Curtis tried to move but his body refused to respond. "Dad," she said more sharply. The pain expanded. He smelled dirt and the sweet scent of Melody's hair.

Curtis loved that clean smell of shampoo, sun, and sweat that only children possessed. He heard a gurgling noise and realized the sound had come from his throat. Again, Melody wiggled under him. He thought she was pressing against her shoulder, urging him to move, but he wasn't sure. It was becoming hard to breathe. His eyes were closed, but he could still see dim light through the lids. The light began to recede around the edges. He wondered just where his plan had gone wrong. Curtis forced himself to take one more gurgling breath then all was dark.

28

Rochelle

———◇———

"E verything's done, at least for tonight," said Alicia. "Thanks for all your help."

"You're welcome," said Rochelle, "and let me know if you need help tomorrow."

Alicia looked exhausted but satisfied. Close by, her son and daughter played a game of hacky sack, using their feet to pitch a multicolored bag back and forth. Melody stood to one side watching and soon Alicia's children invited her to join in their play.

"Go home. You look exhausted," said Rochelle, "although the kids look like they have energy left."

"They'll be asleep before we get home. I hope. Come on you two, time to go." Alicia's daughter picked up the hacky sack bag and they followed their mom.

Rochelle turned to Lucia. "It's good to see you again."

Lucia acted like she hadn't heard. She had watched the children play. After they left, Lucia surveyed the park. She looked even thinner and wearier then she did the last time Rochelle saw her. If was if a breeze could blow her out of the loose-fitting shirt and pants.

Rochelle wondered if Lucia had gone back to work yet at the beef processing plant. The managers had little empathy for events in their workers' lives outside the walls of the building. If something happened—the death of a family member, for instance—and the employee needed more time off, well, there was always someone else eager to take their place waiting outside the gate. Rochelle tried again.

"So, are you doing okay?"

Melody had gone to the drinking fountain for a drink. She came back, scuffing her shoes through the dirt. She looked at the clock mounted on the park pole.

Lucia watched Melody, ignoring Rochelle's question.

"I heard they arrested the boys who shot her," said Rochelle.

"Yeah, that's good, but it's not enough. Those damn gooks, they come to our town, take our jobs. My family's been here for fifteen years.

We paid our dues, but no, the government don't make them people pay. Now they take my Marcela too."

Jim had been accurate in his depiction of Lucia as an angry porcupine, quick to display her quills.

"Still, I'm glad you came. Did someone call you, let you know we were honoring Marcela?"

"I came on my own. No one asked me to come because they don't want to know the truth," said Lucia. She glared at Rochelle.

In the park, the few people who'd remained folded their lawn chairs and drifted toward their cars.

Rochelle couldn't think of anything else to say. Lucia had not processed her grief enough that she could open herself to anyone or anything other than hatred.

Enough of this night. Enough of this woman. Rochelle said goodbye and started toward to her apartment. Her feet ached and she longed for a bath. At the street, she looked around one last time to see if she could locate Jim. What she saw, instead, was Curtis and Colonel Duc walking toward Lucia.

"What the hell?"

Rochelle saw Lucia turn in the direction of Curtis and Colonel Duc and stiffen when she spotted them. The old colonel halted. Curtis took hold of his elbow, prompting him forward.

What, for God's sake, was Curtis thinking? Rochelle started toward Duc and Curtis, wanting to deflect them away from Lucia. She stole a look at Lucia and saw she had reached a hand into her purse. Then Lucia pulled out a pistol, grasped it in both hands, and aimed it at the colonel. The colonel had eyes on Lucia, but Curtis was focused on his daughter walking toward him. That's when he noticed Lucia was holding a gun.

"Melody," Curtis yelled, and ran toward his daughter.

"No, Lucia, don't," shouted Rochelle.

There was an explosion and then another. A uniformed officer tackled Lucia.

Rochelle ran to where Duc and Curtis lay on the ground. She saw the colonel rise and heard a keening sound. Curtis was motionless on the ground, a red stain spreading across his back. Rochelle saw one small hand came out from underneath Curtis and push at his shoulder.

"Oh hell, damn it," Rochelle said.

Jim appeared. He pushed Curtis over so Melody could scramble out from beneath her dad.

Rochelle, her heart rapidly beating, went to help Colonel Duc, but her eyes stayed locked on Jim and Curtis. Jim rolled Curtis onto his back, but the man didn't stir. He started CPR.

Melody screamed, "Daddy! Daddy!" over and over.

Another officer came to Rochelle and Duc to see if the colonel was hurt. He was shaken but Rochelle didn't see any injuries.

"We need paramedics and more officers. Now," said another officer into his radio.

"Mark, get over here, help me do CPR," Jim shouted.

"Check her out," Jim said, this time to Rochelle. He jerked his head toward Melody. "She's got blood all over her."

Rochelle guided Melody several feet away so she wouldn't see what was happening, "Hush, baby, they're working on your dad. Here, let me look you over, make sure you're okay. Hush now, baby."

Rochelle ran her hands first over the girl's front and then her back checking to see if she had been hit too. She didn't find any wounds and the girl didn't act like she was injured. The blood must have come from her father's wounds. Melody stared at the activity around Curtis. "Daddy, daddy," she said, the scream now reduced to a whimper. Rochelle wrapped her arms around Melody, using her body to shield the girl from what was going on behind her—Jim pushing rhythmically on Curtis' chest, the officer, Mark, blowing into his mouth, a widening circle of blood.

Sirens sounded in the distance. Rochelle stole a look at Jim. The expression on his face, when he paused to let the other man breathe into Curtis' mouth, confirmed what Rochelle already knew—it was too late. She pressed Melody's head tight against her breast and stroked her hair.

29

Rochelle

Rochelle rolled a pair of white shorts and tucked them inside the suitcase. It was hot in the apartment, so she gathered her hair and twisted it into a knot at the nape of her neck. She opened the apartment's front window to let in the cool morning breeze.

Across the street, not much was left of the flowers and other items people had placed at a memorial for Curtis. Except for the absence of stuffed animals, the collection with its crosses, flowers, photos, and R.I.P signs reminded Rochelle of Marcela's display. Was that really just a month ago? So much had happened since then.

She returned to the bedroom and pulled a dress from the closet. There was a mirror attached to the back of the closet door and Rochelle held the dress against her, turning first left, then right, to check the reflection. The red dress made her face look pale. She hung the dress back in the closet and pulled a different one from its hanger. That was better. The silvery blue in this dress didn't pull the color from her cheeks.

She added a pair of worn athletic shoes to the suitcase, zipped it closed, and went to the bathroom to pack the travel bag she used for toiletries and cosmetics.

So many of the Kingston residents had showed up at Curtis' funeral that they had to position speakers outside the Methodist Church so the overflow crowd could listen to the funeral ceremony. Rochelle sat with Alicia, Susie Nguyen, and Dr. Kline's widow behind the Myerson family. The surviving Myerson family wasn't large: a brother and his wife, their four half-grown children, and a few assorted cousins.

An older couple sat on one side of Amy. Amy's parents, Rochelle guessed. Melody, on the other side, buried her head in her mother's shoulder and refused to look at the flower-draped casket stationed in front of the altar. Occasionally, Rochelle saw Melody lift her head and observe the people behind her. Once, she looked at Rochelle and lifted her hand in a sad wave of acknowledgement. The girl's expression was vacant. Only her clenched hand, twisted in Amy's hair, revealed her emotions.

Rochelle hoped the girl was seeing a counselor. Strange how grief affected people differently. Lucia couldn't get past the anger, twisting the sorrow to strike out at anyone she perceived had a hand in the death of her daughter. It was hard to know if Lucia had aimed the pistol at Curtis or, in trying to rescue Melody, Curtis inadvertently caught the shot meant for Duc, the grandfather Lucia judged responsible for the actions of his grandson.

There was Melody, whose grief manifested in a refusal to acknowledge that her father lay entombed in a casket. Rochelle thought about her own grief after Eduardo died. Her response had been to flee Miami, escape any reminders of their nights on his motorcycle racing as if the demons of fate chased them. She was doing the same thing now, wasn't she, fleeing this dry town where the best efforts to remake the community into a better place seem to have turned to dust.

Emily Kline told her, as they sat together at the funeral, that her late husband and Curtis had followed their dream to make the world a better place. No doubt her husband had. Rochelle wondered about the truth of it for Curtis. In the measure of one's life, did intent count or was it only fruition of that intent that marked a tally on Saint Peter's tablet at the gates of heaven?

Rochelle shook her hair from its knot and brushed it smooth. She added the brush to the pink travel carrier and latched it. It took two trips to carry the luggage and her cup of iced tea outside to the Toyota Corolla. After the cases were loaded into the truck and the glass of tea set in the cup holder, she went back to the shop for one last check to make sure the air conditioning was off and the closed sign hung in its proper place at the window.

Rochelle exited through the front door of the shop, the bell sounding lonely when she pulled it shut behind her. Rochelle surveyed the quiet street before walking over to the community center to tell Alicia she was temporarily closing the shop.

"Are there any vigil plans for Curtis?" Rochelle asked Alicia.

Alicia shook her head, vigorously, "If someone wants to have one then fine, but I don't want any part of a vigil ever again."

"I saw in the newspaper that they want to rename the park where Curtis died the Gomez-Myerson Park," said Rochelle. She watched Alicia for a reaction. Alicia cocked her eyebrows. She stared out the glass door, her thoughts far away.

Finally, Alicia said, "I heard that too. Ironic, isn't it, the two of them forever linked like that."

"It is," Rochelle said. She couldn't think of anything else to say. "I'd better get going."

"I guess that's a good thing, right?" Alicia said.

It took Rochelle a minute to realize Alicia's thoughts were still on the park's proposed name.

"You mean renaming it the Gomez-Myerson Park?" She thought back to just after Curtis' shooting. Rochelle had sat with her arms around a trembling Melody in the hospital waiting room waiting for her mother to arrive. She saw hospital signs that identified the rooms in three languages—English, Spanish, and Vietnamese. Curtis' funeral included audience members from all factions, and Susie Nguyen's husband and Roger Munoz served as pallbearers. And didn't the newspaper report that the zoo planned to add an Asian exhibit with Red Pandas and Mutjak deer. Strangely shaped fruits, exotic spices, Asian vegetables, and hot dried peppers were common now in the grocery stores.

"Yes," Rochelle said, "that will be a good thing. So we won't forget."

Alicia stepped forward and embraced Rochelle.

The move surprised Rochelle, and it surprised her even more when she felt a tear slid from her eye and drop onto her cheek. She hugged Alicia back, breathed in the floral scent of her shampoo.

"You'll be back, won't you?" asked Alicia, after she released Rochelle and stepped back. There were tears in Alicia's eyes too. She wiped them with the sleeve of her blouse.

"Yes," said Rochelle, even though she wasn't sure.

Rochelle had one last goodbye to make before she left. She had just placed a bouquet of white silk roses in the vase beside Angelina's gravestone when she heard a sound behind her. She knew who it was.

"Morning, Jim," she said, not turning around.

Jim walked up behind her and wrapped his arms around her shoulders. He rested his chin against her head.

"You really are leaving then?" he asked.

"Yes, for a while."

"Where are you going?"

"To visit my aunt and uncle in Miami." She sighed. "Then, I'm not sure." Rochelle had called a couple of sex reassignment clinics and read their brochures but was still conflicted about having the procedure. Jim accepted, relished, the way she was now. Did she feel the same way about him, or had her life become a boggy mire that both soothed and made it hard to move forward.

"Are you going to check out that clinic in New York you talked about?" Jim asked, his face still buried in her hair.

She turned, put her hands on each side of Jim's face, and kissed him on the lips. Then she tilted down his head and kissed his forehead.

"Yes, I'm going to talk with them. But I don't know, yet, what I'll do."

She pressed her index finger against his chest then used the finger to circle the button on his shirt and move down until it reached a spot between his belly and his belt. She watched his face and saw first relief, then uncertainty, and at last longing.

Jim wrapped his around Rochelle and pulled her to him. "I love you, Rochelle. I know I don't say it often, but I do."

"You big, handsome lug," she said, in the throaty voice she knew he loved. She continued, this time in a serious tone. "I love you too. You know that. Whatever I decide, it will be something that both of us," she pointed to Jim and herself, "can live with."

She watched Jim in the Corolla's rearview mirror as she drove toward the cemetery's exit. She watched him stroll back to his own car. When she could no longer see him, Rochelle clicked the seatbelt into its lock and set her course. The days were becoming shorter as summer slid toward fall, but if traffic was light, she could make Tulsa by nightfall.

The End

Questions for Discussion:

1) The novel was narrated from the point of view of two very different characters. How did that enhance or distract from the story? Did it provide greater insight into the problems experienced when different cultures move into a new community?

2) The story was set in the 1980s. What if it were set in the present day? Would the outcome be different?

3) The author killed off Curtis, one of the main characters. What are your thoughts about doing that? Would you write the ending differently? If so, what would it be?

4) The character, Rochelle, left town still undecided about having the surgery to finish the transition to female. What do you think about leaving that matter undecided?

5) As a reader, have you experienced moving into a new city or country where the culture (language, customs, dress, lifestyle) was different? What can community leaders do to make you feel accepted?

6) The novel was based on an actual situation experienced in the author's hometown when immigrants from other countries, as well as refugees from the Vietnam Conflict, were recruited to work in a beef processing plant. The plant received tax advantages for the hirings. Have you experienced a similar situation in a community where you lived? How did it play out?

About the Author

Connie Beckett is the author of *Kingmaker and the Scribe, Murder at the Tindari, Hidden Rooms, Secret Spaces* and the Gwen Lindstrom mystery series. She writes middle-grade fantasy under the pen, Teter Keyes, including the Deidra Ann Adventure series. She resides in northeast Kansas with two cats and a demanding dog.

www.conniebeckett.net